# jane jones:

# WORST. VAMPIRE. EVER.

# jane jones:
# WORST. VAMPIRE. EVER.

by CAISSIE ST. ONGE

EMBER

New York

Text copyright © 2011 by Caissie St. Onge
Cover design by Ellice M. Lee

All rights reserved. Published in the United States by Ember, an imprint of Random House Children's Books, a division of Random House, Inc., New York.

Ember and the colophon are trademarks of Random House, Inc.

Visit us on the Web! www.randomhouse.com/teens

Educators and librarians, for a variety of teaching tools, visit us at www.randomhouse.com/teachers

*Library of Congress Cataloging-in-Publication Data*
St. Onge, Caissie.
Jane Jones, worst. Vampire. Ever. / Caissie St. Onge. — 1st Ember ed.
    p. cm.
Summary: Vampire Jane Jones, neither rich nor beautiful nor popular, is tired of struggling with an overprotective mother and an allergy to blood, but suddenly two boys, one vampire and one human, are interested in her, and she has learned of a possible cure for her condition.
ISBN 978-0-375-86891-7 (trade pbk.: alk. paper) —
ISBN 978-0-375-96891-4 (lib. bdg.: alk. paper) — ISBN 978-0-375-89976-8 (ebook)
[1. Vampires—Fiction. 2. Self-esteem—Fiction. 3. Popularity—Fiction. 4. Mothers and daughters—Fiction. 5. High schools—Fiction. 6. Schools—Fiction.] I. Title.
PZ7.S77437Jan 2011
[Fic]—dc22
2010022074

RL: 5.6

Printed in the United States of America
10 9 8 7 6 5 4 3 2 1
First Ember Edition 2011

For my father, Michael, a guy who loved a good story

jane jones:

WORST.
VAMPIRE.
EVER.

# one

**"Oh my God, you guys. I am sooooo wasted.** Did you see me? I was totally chugging, and now I'm, like . . . totally wasted!"

Astrid Hoffman was one of my classmates at my new school, Port Lincoln High. So far, what I'd learned about her was that she was wealthy and confident and lovelier than any girl in the sophomore class. In fact, she was the most poised and best-looking girl in the entire school, from what I could tell, wasted or not. Even heavily intoxicated, even kind of slurring and drooling with her thick, glossy brown curls falling over her glassy green eyes, she was a looker. She made me sick.

Astrid turned her half-lidded gaze to me. "Jane! Jaaaaa-aaaane. It's your turn. Have a little drinky drink, new girl!" Everyone around the bonfire cheered and someone shoved me in Astrid's direction.

I nervously shook my head. Actually, if I'm being

honest, I probably spastically shook my head. "Uh, no. No, thanks. I don't really . . ."

"Aw, Jane, what's the matter? Your mommy won't let you?" Astrid teased. Then the playful look slipped from her face, replaced by an expression of menacing threat. "I'm not asking, Jane, I'm telling you. Drink!"

Astrid bared her teeth at me as everyone around us started chanting, "Drink! Drink! Drink! Drink!" So this, I recalled bitterly, is what peer pressure feels like. In the past, I'd learned to avoid peer pressure by avoiding as much contact as possible with my so-called peers, but on this night, I found myself understanding how things get out of hand. All of a sudden, it was like *Lord of the Flies* up in there and I found myself in not so great a position to resist.

I inched toward Astrid, my mind racing. Funny how a moment is enough time for your whole life to pass before your eyes but not long enough to think of a decent plan for escaping a crappy situation. Knowing there was no way to get out of it, I knelt beside her and said, "Okay, I'll drink."

"Good girl," she cooed, winking as she hefted the pale, bare leg of Ian Holcomb into my lap. There were two small holes in the soft, white pit of his knee, ringed with what looked almost like a lipstick kiss at the bottom of a love letter, but in the shade of his own blood.

The rest of Ian was facedown in the dirt, dozing happily, I presume. He was also wasted, but in the more traditional human sense. Probably on his dad's vodka and his mom's sugar-free Red Bull. Whatever he'd been drinking that night, Astrid had made it a point to corner Ian and thank him personally for inviting her to such an awesome rager. Then she made it a further point to lean in really close to his chest and say right into his ear, "I'm having an awesome time." Then, when Ian suggested that they go out for some air, she responded by saying, "That would be awesome." I have to admit, what Astrid lacked in vocabulary skills, she made up for in cunning. Now she was hosting her own little party by the side of the state road behind the Holcombs' property, and the bar was fully stocked with Ian's elevated blood-alcohol level.

As I bent over poor, dumb Ian's popliteal artery, I asked myself two questions: *What the hell am I even doing here?* and *How am I gonna make this look good?*

I pushed my glasses up my nose, then shoved my face right up against Ian's leg and clamped my mouth on a spot that looked clean. I closed my eyes and did my best to imitate the rapture I was supposed to be feeling as I sank my fangs into the flesh of the JV football captain. Only, I wasn't sinking my fangs into anything. I was completely faking it and I might have gotten away with it, too, if I hadn't gone in for that one last convincing slurp. That was when Ian, in his stupor, sort of snorted and jerked the way you do when you dream that you're falling. The sudden motion must have spiked his blood pressure for just a second, but one second was all it took for arterial blood spray to hit me full in the face. Horrified, I dropped Ian's leg as my hands flew up, too late to block the gruesome mist. My cheeks were slick. The lenses of my glasses were covered with sticky, warm drops. I tore them off and rubbed furiously at my eyes with the sleeve of my favorite flannel shirt.

"Jane!" Astrid howled. "What an idiot. You should see your face! You look totally hilarious." Oh, I'm sure I did look totally hilarious. We've all seen *Carrie*, right? Everybody knows that there's nothing more hysterically funny than a teenager suddenly and unexpectedly drenched in blood. Unfortunately, in my case, I didn't have the telekinesis necessary to make a tree fall on Astrid to shut her up. Unfortunately, I was having a difficult time even standing up.

As all the vampire kids circled around to get a better look at me, I realized something very bad had just happened. Whether it had dripped into my mouth as I sat there slack-jawed or whether it had aerosolized and gone up my nose, somehow I had ingested at least a tiny amount of Ian's blood. While I may have looked bad, I was about to look a whole lot worse. See, like it doesn't suck enough to be a teenager who's a vampire who's a complete dork, I also have this other problem. I'm blood-intolerant.

Within seconds I could feel hot hives rising on my skin. Panic set in as I felt my throat start to close, and my breathing became shallow, raspy gasps. Weird that someone most people might think of as technically dead needs to keep breathing, but I can assure you that breathing is something I very much enjoy and wanted to continue doing. I scrabbled on my hands and knees over to where everyone was standing and gawking, searching the ground for my backpack. Although the laughter didn't die down as much as I would have liked it to, it had at least taken on a more nervous and confused tone.

After what felt like minutes, I found my bag and yanked open the front zipper. With shaking hands I extracted what looked like a pen but was actually a small syringe that contained a dose of medication similar to what human cancer patients receive during chemotherapy. I ripped the cap off with my teeth and plunged the needle through my jeans into my scrawny thigh. Almost instantly, the chemical went to work, seeking out the drop of Ian's blood, wherever it had gone inside me, and killing off the red blood cells, rendering it harmless to me and neutralizing my terrible reaction. But besides saving my life, or unlife or whatever, that stuff also comes with the side effect of knocking me the heck out.

I knew everyone was standing around me, looking down on me, literally for once. The last thing I remember hearing as my eyes rolled up into my head was, "Holy ▓▓▓. She's allergic to blood? What a freak." The last thing I remember thinking was, *When a group of freaks are calling you a freak, it's pretty freaking bad.*

When I came around again, I had no idea how much time had passed. I could make out Ian's shape on the ground a few feet from me, and it looked like he was still out cold. I reasoned that, all things considered, he might be in better shape than I was. I pushed myself up onto my elbows and tried to focus my eyes. It seemed like mostly everyone was still standing around the dying fire, but my little scene had definitely been a downer. When I swiveled my head around to make sure my neck still worked, I noticed the silhouette of someone sitting near me.

"You're up." The voice was low and scratchy and I couldn't even begin to place it.

"I picked up your glasses. I didn't want them to get stepped on. I cleaned them off, as well as I could." The blurry figure moved toward me and, rather than handing them to me, just went ahead and gently placed the frames right on my face. As he stepped back, I saw that it was Timothy Hunt, a vampire from the junior class who ran with Astrid's crowd.

It dawned on me that the reason I couldn't place his voice was because this was the first time I had ever heard him speak. Sure, I had seen him plenty of times. I mean, he was kind of hard not to notice with his carelessly floppy honey-colored hair and his dark-yet-luminous blue eyes and his perfectly pouty pout. If you were into the whole emo-broody thing, which I knew a lot of girls both vampire and human were, I guess you'd probably look at him every chance you got. But like I said, prior to this night, I'd been pretty good at skipping things like eye contact and conversation. Now all I could do was make eye contact. I mean, why make myself look less stupid at this point, right?

"You're welcome," he said. I know he definitely smiled at me, but the thing is, I wasn't sure if it was a friendly let's-be-friends kind of smile or more of an I'm-laughing-at-you-and-not-with-you kind of smile. I mean, he had done a nice thing by picking up my glasses, but considering all that had just gone down and who his friends were, the chances were decent that I was being mocked. If being a vampire had been a sport, Timothy would have been the captain of the varsity vampire team, but I think we can all admit that being well loved doesn't necessarily equal being lovable. I tried to keep my guard up, just in case.

"Thanks. I . . . Thanks."

Timothy tipped an imaginary hat to me and stood. My bespectacled eyes followed him all the way up. I'm sure my mouth was hanging open too. So much for that guard of mine.

"Do you need a hand getting up, or should you—" Timothy was interrupted by Celeste, one of Astrid's dearest friends and loyal henchwomen.

"Hey, Lame." I guess she'd nicknamed me Lame because it kind of rhymes with Jane. It wasn't the cleverest insult I'd ever been subjected to, but it would do in a pinch. "We thought you were dying so we called your house. Your mother's on her way."

"Oh, God," I moaned under my breath. This evening just kept getting better and better. I briefly considered running into the woods and trying to find my own way home. I figured maybe I could play dumb about the phone call and convince my parents that it had been some prank. I had been the victim of pranks in other towns we'd lived in, TP'ed trees and the occasional flaming bag of dog doo. But when I saw Celeste toss my cell phone down on top of my backpack, I realized that because none of them had my home phone number, they'd used my cell phone to call my folks. I wouldn't be able to explain away why it had been my number that had popped up on my home's caller ID. Besides, before I could even fully stand, we all heard a rustling and crashing through the brush, and someone rushed toward us from the nearby road.

"Lord have mercy, Jane, is that you?" My mother, dressed in a coat not quite long enough to conceal an old blue cotton nightgown and not nearly long enough to cover her bare legs and bedroom slippers, ran toward me and squeezed me in a frantic maternal embrace. I stiffened like a humiliated piece of timber. "Sweetheart, I was scared to death. Your friends called and said you'd fainted. Are you okay?"

Then a few things happened in a rapid domino effect. As my mother buried her face in my hair, her own keen sense of vampire smell kicked in. Her head reared back and suddenly, rather than embracing me, she was holding me at arm's length with an incredulous look on her face. "Jane Jones, is that blood I smell?" Before I could answer, out of the corner of her eye she noticed Ian, still dead to the world, with the right leg of his jeans rolled up past his knee.

"What in the world is going on here?" my mother shouted at everyone still standing around. "Would somebody like to explain this to me?"

Astrid snickered. "He was having a party. He's drunk."

"Oh, I see, so you all thought that you'd feed off him and get a little tipsy yourselves, right? Did you ever stop to think that someone might notice he was missing from his own party? Did you ever stop to think that when you're drunk, you're careless and that you risk exposing yourselves and the whole . . . community?"

"We were going to put him back when we were done." Astrid shuffled her expensive shoes in the dead pine needles. "Don't have a freak-out."

For the first time this whole evening, I was really with Astrid. If my mom could find it in her heart not to have a freak-out just this once, I would be truly grateful. No such luck, though.

"Aren't you the Hoffman girl? Your parents are going to hear from me. Oh, all of your parents are going to hear from me."

"Mrs. Jones, I'm sure my parents would love to hear from you," said Astrid. "When they get back. They're at our home in Germany until after the New Year." Astrid leveled a gaze at my mother that didn't contain a hint of remorse or fear. It was strange. On the one hand, my mother was the adult in this situation. On the other hand, it was more than likely that Astrid, though having the appearance and temperament of a teenager, had actually been on this earth for hundreds of years longer than my mother, depending on when she'd been bitten and infected with vampiritis. Either way, she certainly wasn't intimidated by my mother's threat. Neither was Celeste.

"Yeah, Mrs. Jones, I'm sure my parents would love to hear from you too, but they died from bubonic plague." It was probably true, but it was difficult to feel pity for an orphan who was shaking with laughter at the mention of her own deceased family.

Realizing that her outrage was not having the sobering effect she'd intended, my mother turned on me. "And you, Jane. What were you thinking? You know you can't drink blood."

"I didn't mean to, I . . ." But you know how it is when your mom has something to say. She's going to say it.

"Didn't mean to? Are you saying it was an accident?"

"Well, it wasn't an accident, I was . . ."

"You were displaying incredibly poor judgment. Not to mention what you let happen to this young man." She gestured to Ian, who had now balled himself up in a cozy-looking fetal position in the chilly September night air.

"Boys," she said to Timothy and another guy I sometimes saw at Celeste's locker. I mouthed a silent prayer that she wouldn't do anything to further embarrass me in front of Timothy. "Do you think you can help this fellow back to his house without attracting much attention?"

"Yes, ma'am," Timothy replied.

"Good, see that you do. And no more feeding from him. Put him in bed, but don't undress him. With any luck, he'll be so preoccupied with his hangover when he wakes up, he won't notice any fang marks on his leg."

The boys stooped to hoist Ian up. They draped his flaccid arms around their shoulders and dragged him to his feet, but hesitated, awaiting further orders from my mother.

For the moment, it seemed like she didn't have any. It seemed like she'd said her piece and was ready to let everyone go their separate ways. I'd survived an excruciating social event, a toxic blood reaction, and near death by parental mortification, and I was ready to call it a night. Too bad for me that my mother wasn't, just yet.

"The rest of you should get to your houses," she instructed. "Stick close to the road, but stay in the woods so that you won't be seen. And Jane, I'd better get you home ASAP. I'm guessing you're in for one hell of a case of diarrhea tonight."

If it weren't for the fact that I had technically not been alive for several decades, I would have died of humiliation right there.

# two

**"What were you thinking, Josephine?"** She tore open the glove box in front of me and grabbed a bottle of hand sanitizer, which she furiously pumped into her palm and then mine. I opted not to remark on the absurdity of that precaution. You can't catch your death much worse than we already had. I rubbed my hands together until she bellowed, "Well?"

I had been yelled at so many times in our old Volvo station wagon, but I could tell this session was going to be particularly searing. My first clue was that my mother used my real first name, Josephine, the one she gave me when I was born, the name I had before I even knew what a vampire was.

"I was just . . ." I had started speaking before my mother was finished.

"I mean, why would you put yourself at risk like that? You could have died . . . well, not *died* died, but how could you do something so stupid?"

I said "I was just . . ." again, but apparently, *I was just* was just not enough to stop Hurricane Ma.

"Not to mention the fact that if that boy had sobered up, you could have been discovered. We could have all been discovered. Did you think of that?" She paused, as if waiting to hear my answer before asking again. Maybe she actually wanted me to participate in this "discussion." "Did you?"

"I didn't think—"

"No, you didn't think," Ma interrupted. "Not for one second, did you?"

"Ma, I didn't really do anything."

"Oh, I don't want to *hear* it! I don't want to hear the excuses! You know what? Just sit there with your mouth shut until we get home."

I would have been totally happy to sit there with my mouth shut for seven years if that's what my mother really wanted. But I knew she didn't. I knew she was about to start right back up again in five, four, three, two—

"I really want to understand what was going through your head. I really want to understand, Jo, why?" That last *why* came out kind of soft. I don't want to give you the impression that my mother was no longer angry with me. It's more like she had exhausted herself with the exertion of tearing me five new ones. Well, she wasn't the only one who had a right to be upset. So now that she'd piped down, I let her have it right back.

"*Why*? You want to know why? Because you *made* me go out with them! You ordered me to call Astrid and ask if I could hang out with all the vampire kids because you were sick of me lying around the house. You made me beg to play their vampire games. And that's what they do, Ma! That's their idea of fun."

"But just because all of them were doing it doesn't mean—"

"Doesn't mean I had to do it too? Ma, you act like I haven't been a teenager for the last seventy-five years. Believe me, I've tried just saying no to peer pressure. It doesn't always work. Especially if your peers happen to be a-holes." My voice was shaking with emotion, but I had more to say.

"You're the one who put me at risk, Ma. Because even though all those vampire kids share a secret, you knew I had something else that I would have liked to keep secret from them. And now they all know, and even if I live another thousand years, I will never live it down. I'm a mutant among mutants."

"Jo . . ."

"It's Jane, Ma. At least for the next four years until we move again. In fact, you can call me Lame—it's what my 'friends' call me." From the look on my mother's face, I could tell I'd made her feel bad. Well, good. She was such a hypocrite, trying to tell me how to run my social life, or lack of social life, when she wouldn't be caught undead hobnobbing with any of the adults in the local vampire community. Sure, *no* matter where we lived, we were always among others like us, because there is a thriving vampire community in just about any American town, and unfortunately our numbers seem to be growing all the time. But my mother obviously didn't trust any of them. And for good reason. So why should she expect me to be any different?

"I know how difficult this is, Jane," she said. "I just thought things would be easier if you had some friends in your new school."

I didn't feel like really putting the screws to her, but the truth is, she didn't know at all how difficult it was. She'd only ever gone to a one-room schoolhouse, and only until the eighth grade, before leaving to help out on her family farm. Then she married my dad and they had their own farm to take care of. I remember that wasn't going so well before everything . . . changed for us. So, while she's no stranger to difficulty, she has no idea what it's like for me, a former farmer's daughter, now a vampire, attending her fourteenth high school in a town that happens to be filled with mortal as well as supernatural jerks.

"I know what a great girl you are, Jane. Not everyone can be popular, but I know that if you just tried a little harder, you could make a few good friends."

"Don't be so sure, Ma. The vampires may have to put up with me, but the regular kids . . . it's like they don't even see me."

"I bet you're selling yourself short, honey."

"Ma, you know the group of super-nerdy kids who are obsessed with vampire novels and walk around the mall wearing capes? Even *they* won't let me sit with them at lunch." I knew I sounded pitiful now, but it was true. It was also kind of funny when I said it out loud like that. I guess it sounded funny to my mother too, because she covered her mouth to try to hide her smile before I could see it. Then she snorted.

"I'm sorry. I don't mean to laugh."

"It's okay. It's funny. It's ironic. I mean, people always say they're doing something ironically and it's supposed to be funny, but usually it's not really ironic at all. But this is genuine irony!" Now we were both LOLing and I noticed that despite our cool breath, we'd managed to fog the Volvo's windows just a bit. I wiped my hand on the glass.

"I guess we'd better get home before a policeman thinks we're a couple of kids out parking," she said.

Oh, God. Did she really just say that out loud? Ma can always be counted on to take a pretty decent moment and put a stop to it by saying something creepy or corny. This time was a two-fer.

We drove home in relative silence. It took a good fifteen minutes, because we lived clear across town from the Holcomb compound. Port Lincoln is a scenic town on the coast of Connecticut. The old roads are lined with old mansions built with old money. The new developments are dotted with new mansions built with new money. There's a gorgeous river with a rowing club and the only requirements to join are that you're gorgeous and interested in rowing.

On the other side of that river, over a quaint little bridge and in the armpit of the highway and the train tracks that can take you to New York City, there's a little neighborhood. It's technically in Port Lincoln, but the houses are small and old. Not in the old mansion way, more in the worn and outdated way. That's where we lived. I don't want to make it sound like it was skid row, because the truth is that even though the houses were straight out of the seventies, they were all in good repair, with washed curtains and lawns striped light and dark green due to frequent mowings. My theory is that was because my neighbors were the handymen, housekeepers, and landscapers who catered to the rest of the town. Of course, it's only a theory because I didn't really know any of my neighbors. I didn't really plan to. What was the point, when in a few short years, I'd have a whole new set?

We pulled into our driveway, and I trudged behind my mother up to the front door. That's another thing about vampires. We can't fly. We don't have superspeed. We drive cars and we trudge when we're tired. I was so tired.

My mother unlocked the door and flipped on the dim hallway light. She brushed my lank bangs out of my eyes and said, "Try to be quiet going upstairs. Your brother is asleep."

I nodded and padded up the carpeted staircase to my small, dark room. My hand searched and found the light switch. From the six recessed fixtures in my ceiling, huge 800-watt bulbs—like the ones used in sunlamps—hummed to life. I know you've heard the stories of how sunlight will destroy a vampire as soon as it touches his skin. In real life, direct sun is more like an irritant to vampires. If we bake in it, we get burned, just like you. Okay, we might crisp up a *little* faster than the living, but then, melanomas aren't really an issue for us either. So we cover up, we wear SPF 100, and we stay in the shade. Everyone just thinks we're Irish or something. And since we try to exist in the regular world, most of us keep normal hours, going to work and school during the day and sleeping at night. Vampires need the heat generated by the UV lamps to help us fight our bodies'—um, our *corpses'*—natural unnatural instincts to stay awake after sundown.

Of course, I realize this isn't the greenest practice and the irony that I may be contributing to the eventual destruction of the Earth when I'm someone who will probably need the Earth for kind of a long time is not lost on me. Plus I feel guilty about our insanely high electric bills, especially since I require extra wattage, due to my unfortunate condition. The glow coming from my ceiling would have been too much for even the most tanorexic human. I quickly double-checked the light-blocking blinds we'd installed so that curious neighbors wouldn't drop by to ask why daylight was radiating from our house, then I opened the curtains surrounding my canopy bed and flopped down in the warm darkness, exhausted.

I had closed my eyes for only one second before my mom's head poked into my lair. "Are you hungry? I could defrost a little something for you."

A little something, in my case, would be a drop of Bombay blood. It's the rarest blood type in the world. Lots of people think the rarest blood type is AB negative, because not many people have it, but Bombay blood is even scarcer. It has something to do with things called phenotypes and antigens. My younger brother, Zachary, could explain the exact science to you. He's, like, a scientific genius even though he only looks ten. What I do know is that Bombay blood type was discovered in India in 1952 and I first tasted it in 1968 when my mother got her hands on some to test my brother's theory that I could tolerate it. Fortunately, he was correct, because prior to that, after a few scary reactions to regular blood, I never fed on anything. That's something else about vampires you might not know. We don't absolutely need to drink blood to live. With only a few exceptions, nothing can really kill us, no matter what kind of rough shape we're in. However, we do need blood to be healthy, but only a drop or two every day. Of course, there are vampires who can't control their urge to have more than a drop or two . . . or two thousand. When you hear about a person being drained by a vampire, it's because they were unlucky enough to meet a vampire with a real drinking problem. Since the only blood I can feed on is extremely precious—found in just four people out of every million—I can never afford to get that greedy. I eat much less frequently than others of my kind and I've existed off of the same bag of black-market donor blood for at least ten years. Yes, it was more expensive than I could even wrap my mind around, but it's been a decade since we've had to go "grocery shopping" for me.

I shook my head no at Ma's offer of an impromptu snack, and she leaned in to kiss my chilly cheek with her cool lips before she turned and left for the warmth of her own bedroom. It was hard enough for us to sleep at night, but I knew it was even more difficult for her since my father had taken a job as a night quality-control manager at the Fresh Meadow Farms cookie and cracker plant in the next town over. It seemed like an ideal gig for a vampire, except for the fact that he had no use for the one semi-decent job perk of unlimited free cookies and crackers. In fact, the smell of those things baking made him pretty nauseated. But who knows, that might have been the case even if he'd still been human. Fresh Meadow Farms cookies and crackers are basically made of sawdust and glue.

There was a time when my family would have been grateful to have any free food at our disposal, no matter how repugnant it was. I remember our sad little farm on the Oklahoma panhandle. I remember my father planting wheat, even though the crop had failed the year before. I remember all of us being so hungry that we thought about eating the skeletal old milk cow we had loved like a pet. Then I remember a brown cloud rolling across the plain and my mother covering our faces with wet rags as our house rattled and filled with something that looked like smoke. When it was over, dust had drifted in front of our door like snow. The cow was dead. The wheat was gone. Both of my parents cried, and so my brother and I cried too. I thought for a while that we would pack up our things and move away after that, but we didn't. My mother just went to work cleaning the house, and my father replanted the wheat. I couldn't help out the way I should have, because I came down with a pretty bad case of pneumonia and almost died. Almost. From what my parents have told me, we were all closer to death than they could admit at the time.

According to Ma, even without me being able to sit up or eat, we had run out of food. We had no livestock and no dry goods and no money or credit to buy even a tin of anything to share. My parents were ashamed, but they agreed that we couldn't go on that way. So my father set out on foot—because he'd never earned enough to buy the horse and carriage he'd planned on getting one day—to ask Mr. and Mrs. Pike if they had anything to spare. The Pikes had just settled in to the house nearest to ours, and I recall my parents being so thrilled to have neighbors. When my father arrived, he found them loading their Model A pickup truck with all of their belongings, saying they were moving on, going to try their luck out West. When my father explained our situation, the Pikes graciously drove him back to our house on their way. Ruth Pike offered to come in and help Ma make a stew out of some of the meat and vegetables she'd packed away for the trip. Turner Pike told my father, "You ain't never had nothing like my Ruthie's stew." It's true. We never had. And we never did either. By the time the Pikes peeled away from our farm, my family was no longer dying of starvation. Also, my family was no longer officially living.

Like I said, I was worse off than anyone because of how sick I was. When I finally came around, my mother, my father, and Zachary were still trying to figure out what in the holy hell had happened to all of them. It wasn't like the Pikes were kind enough to leave an instruction manual. From what they remembered, once Ruth and Turner had been invited across the threshold of our home, it was over within minutes. Ruth bit my father, and when my mother tried to pull her off, she was bitten by someone. My parents couldn't bring themselves to describe what had happened to my brother, but I guessed he'd been somebody's dessert. Nobody ever said what had happened to me either. My father did once tell me that when he woke up, Turner was squeezing drops of blood from Ruth's fingertip into my mother's mouth. When Ruth saw that he was awake, she just said, "Soon you're all gonna feel right fine again." Then they were gone.

At first, we didn't understand what we'd become.

Eventually, though, my parents pieced together memories of the attack with scary stories they'd heard whispered around campfires. They gradually noticed that thoughts of food were slipping away, and the idea of eating something that once made us drool now repulsed us. Even though my parents had never been particularly religious, I remember my mother praying that it was all a mistake. Then I remember her trying to accept it, even saying what a blessing it was, because while we surely would have died from hunger before, now we could stay and keep trying to make the farm work, no matter how many dust storms blew through. She was in some deep denial. Soon it became apparent that even if my father could have planted a successful crop, it wasn't practical for him to be tending fields in the hot sun every day.

Ancient instincts also started kicking in, telling my family that in order to get stronger, we would need to feed like the Pikes had. We were thin and pale and hungry in a way that was altogether different from the way we had been hungry before. When we thought about eating, our sharp canine teeth protruded like animal fangs. As a family, we made a pact that we would feed as sparingly as possible. We wouldn't kill anyone and we wouldn't turn anyone like we'd been turned.

It wasn't long after that I discovered my problem. I

mean, besides the problem of being a vampire. I vanted to suck blood, I just vasn't able to vithout nearly croaking. While my family cooked up schemes and tricks for dining on human blood as ethically as they could, I just existed, thinner and paler and hungrier than ever.

The problem with a vampire thinking about her past is that there's so much past to think about. Once you get started down memory lane, it's hard to stop remembering all the places you've been and all the people you've left behind. My family has been moving to a new town every four years for the past seventy-five years. It's because we have to hide the fact that we're not aging like regular people. I'm not sure exactly what would happen if we just decided to stay put, but I wish that we could. I would even stay here, in this place that I hate, where I will never fit in. I can't think of anything dumber than living forever when every other thing in your life is so temporary.

If I had accepted my mother's offer of a bedtime drop, I might have been able to sleep. My body was so tired, my limbs were rubbery, but my mind wouldn't be quiet. I got out of bed and powered down the sunlamps. I made my way across my darkened room, sat at my desk, and opened my laptop. I logged on to my email account. Don't think I don't understand how sad it is that the highlight of my day is often reading a scam email from a fake Nigerian prince who claims that he needs to borrow money from me in order to make us both rich. I get that it's pathetic, but I set up an email account because even pathetic loners need to be reachable in order to join message boards in order to talk with other pathetic loners.

I actually like the Internet, because I can just pretend to be a regular human weirdo there. I belong to one web-ring where all the members are video-gamers and another one where everyone is a huge fan of this particular reality show. Honestly, I don't give a rat's tiny heinie about either of those things, but the people are friendly enough and I can talk for a little while without much chance of expos-ing who I am. What I am. Sometimes, on the gamer board, I even get a little flirty with this one guy who's kind of funny. Once, my mom flipped out when she eavesread an exchange between us over my shoulder. She gave me this huge lecture about how the Internet is full of predators who are dangerous, especially to young girls. I completely agreed with her but couldn't resist pointing out that I could, in theory, be considered the predator in this situa-tion. True, a pitiful blood-intolerant vampire, but a gen-uine vampire nonetheless.

When I opened my email, I had four messages. No Nigerian princes, but one alert about a sale at Hot Topic and one offer to sell me some celebrity's secrets for teeth whitening. I briefly wondered if it would work on my fangs before hitting Delete.

The third message was slightly intriguing. When we moved to town, I had set up a Facebook page for myself, with my new alias, Jane Jones. At the time, I was fantasizing about all the new acquaintances I would make in this place. I wasn't really taking into account the fact that after being in high school for decades on end, I had never really associated with anyone who I would want to talk to outside of school. Needless to say, I was surprised when I read, "Eli Matthews has added you as a friend on Facebook. We need to confirm that you know Eli Matthews in order for you to be friends." Eli Matthews was a kid whose name I thought I recognized from my American history class. Maybe. We might have had some other classes together too, but I wasn't sure. If he was who I wasn't 100 percent certain he was, he wasn't exactly noteworthy. Still, he had noticed me, I guess. My hand hovered over my laptop. After the evening's events I wasn't sure how smart it was to establish a relationship with someone at school, no matter how virtual or casual it was. I didn't click Confirm, but I didn't click Ignore or Delete either. The message would be there when I decided what I should do.

The last message was a news alert I had set up for any article or blog post containing the words *vampire* and *cure*.

I had originally set it up with just *vampire*, but thanks to certain movies starring certain ████ teen actors, my in-box was flooded. Once I refined my search to include the word *cure*, the notifications practically dried up. When I did get a hit, it was usually an article in which the two words had nothing to do with each other in context. Occasionally, I'd get a link to some crazy vamp fan fiction. I wasn't expecting much when I clicked on the email or when I clicked on the link contained within. Actually, the website I was taken to didn't say much itself, yet what it did say nearly knocked me off my chair. The headline simply said, "Local Researcher Claims Vampires Exist, and He's Found a Cure for Their Condition."

# three

---

## Local Researcher Claims Vampires Exist, and He's Found a Cure for Their Condition

---

**I scanned the article for what had to be the zillionth time since Friday night.** Of course, I'd printed it out right away so I could fold it up and hide it from my parents. Then I made sure to delete the email and erase my browser history. I had to do it. Like I said, my mom's really into Internet safety, so I'm pretty sure that while I'm at school she looks at all the websites I've been on to see if I'm downloading naked pictures or something. Kind of bizarre considering I'm technically in my early nineties.

In any case, my mom's reaction to finding ▓▓▓▓ on my computer would pale in comparison to what she'd do if she found out that I was researching potential cures for vampirism. It wasn't that my family didn't dream of being

30

cured. Lots of vampires do. It's just that we'd heard the stories of other vampires who'd attempted treatments and the results had been bad. And by bad, I mean fatal. And by fatal, I mean that we'd heard about a few of our kind who went from being undead to totes dead. Whether or not these stories were true is anybody's guess. But it isn't like pharmaceutical companies are spending research money testing drugs to cure a condition most mortals aren't even aware is real. Any vampire who considers a cure must also consider that he's taking his life, such as it is, into his own cold, dead hands. My parents weren't too big on stuff like that.

By now, my printout of the article was all smudged and tattered from my furtively reading it every chance I got over the weekend. Now that I was at school, sitting on the floor in front of my locker, I felt fairly safe just reading it out in the open. When I say "safe," I mean nobody here was interested in me or what I was doing or what I was reading.

"Hey, Jane."

I didn't even have to raise my eyes to know that Timothy Hunt was standing above me. After finally hearing his husky voice, I would never again fail to recognize it. Plus, while I was lying on the ground the night we met, I memorized his shoes. If I had a pulse it would have quickened.

"You feeling a little better?"

I was feeling a lot better than the last time he saw me. I'm sure I was looking at least slightly better too, but I noticed he didn't say, "You're looking a lot better." Still, he was asking how I was feeling, so that had to be a good thing, right? I just needed to not overthink it. Just say yes and thank you and remember to smile.

"Hey, Lame! How's your diarrhea? Was it a hell of a case, like your mom predicted?" I guess Astrid and her traveling band of vampire jerks had seen Timothy talking to me and decided they weren't into it. Even though this was a new school, I was pretty used to this sort of thing. Of the two of us, I felt worse for Timothy. He looked embarrassed. Though when I considered it, the possibility that he was embarrassed to be caught talking with me needled at my brain. Assuming I was correct, my pity for him turned to pity for myself, and my feelings toward him cooled. A little.

"Come on, Tim. We've got to get to health class." Astrid grabbed Timothy by his elbow and pivoted away from me on the toe of her black stiletto knee-high boot. If he looked back, I didn't see it, because I was intently examining my cuticles and chewing my lower lip, hard enough to draw blood, if I'd had any blood to draw. Health class—what a joke. Health class at this school was the same as at any other school I'd ever been to—a glorified study hall "taught" by a coach or PE teacher, and the domain of underachieving students afraid to study a real science like biology or anatomy. I know that on some level, it makes sense for teenage vampires to do the bare minimum to get by. After all, a perfect GPA is something you strive to achieve because of what it could mean for your future. Since all of us are stuck repeatedly living the present over and over, why kill yourself with schoolwork? But on the other hand, class debate and discussion are some of the only outlets I have. I'm smarter than your average high-school vampire and even though it's not cool, I'm true to who I am. The only thing I ever worry about is distinguishing myself too much. I'm pretty sure I could easily graduate among the top ten in my class, but that would bring unwanted attention to and interest in my future, so I've got to pull my academic punches to hang toward the middle of the pack.

The warning bell rang as I stood to open my locker and grab my books for first period. Unlike my classmates, I didn't treat my locker as if it were a three-dimensional scrapbook of celebrities and rock stars I idolized. Actually, if I had to pick an all-time favorite, it would probably be Jimmy Stewart, and I don't think I could have gotten away with pinning up his picture even back in 1945. When it came to my locker, I was strictly pragmatic, but I did hang a small magnetic mirror in there to make sure I didn't look like an absolute troll. Yes, we *can* see our reflections, and mine revealed that the skin on my nose was peeling a bit. I'd run out of the house without carefully applying sunscreen that morning and I'd obviously missed a spot. Luckily, it was a gray September day and if I could steer clear of sitting by a window, further damage might be avoidable.

My first class was AP American history, and it was one of my favorites. Our teacher, Ms. Smithburg, was fresh out of grad school and maybe a little naive, in the best possible way. She thought learning history should be more than just memorizing facts to be tested on later. She wanted us to take what was said in our textbooks with a grain of salt—she definitely was not trying to pretend that Christopher Columbus just happened to find America one day while he was out shopping for spices and that the Native Americans were like, "No, you go ahead. Take our country, please. We insist."

I liked that Ms. Smithburg wanted to hear our thoughts on the long-term implications of the Great Depression, because *I* had plenty of those. I loved that when you stopped by after school to discuss a grade that was a little lower than you thought you deserved, she smiled and said, "Please. I'm off the clock. Call me Charlotte." She treated you as an equal.

I normally sit in the first or second row of a classroom when seats aren't assigned. When you're trying to ride the line between involved and inconspicuous, it's really the place to be. Even in an AP class, anything past the fourth row and you're smack in the middle of what might as well be health class for all of the chatting and flirting and texting that goes on. Today, though, Ms. Smithburg had rearranged our chairs so that they were facing each other in groups of two. My strategy ruined, I at least managed to grab a seat near the front and toward the door, away from any windows or sunbeams that might break through the clouds. The chair across from me was empty as the final bell rang.

"Good morning, good morning, good morning," said Ms. Smithburg. "I trust all of you had a wonderful weekend. So did I, thanks for asking."

Ms. Smithburg waltzed between the odd configuration of desks while passing out packets of stapled papers. "You may be wondering why you're sitting face to face," she said. "Today, we'll be starting our major project for this quarter. Of course, I'm talking about term papers!"

Groans instantly rumbled through the room.

"Now, I know: term papers are the worst. You hate writing them and, frankly, I hate reading them. Which is why I am proposing that we try it this way. You came into class, you spotted a friend and sat down across from them.

Who better than this person you like well enough to sit across from to be your partner for this project?"

I breathed a sigh of relief. I had no problem being the odd person who was unable to pair up for an assignment I could more than handle on my own. In fact, I preferred it that way.

Just as Ms. Smithburg was about to launch into the specifics, the classroom door clicked open. She took the late slip being handed to her by the boy in the doorway and read it. "Mr. Matthews, you are late because you were having your braces tightened. No problem, we were just getting started. Please have a seat across from Ms. Jones." Just like that, the rotten bottom fell out of my day. No, the rotten bottom had fallen out of my whole first term and now the decayed walls were collapsing on me.

Eli Matthews took the seat across from me and his mouthful of tightened braces broke into a weird grin. It was all I could do to keep from putting my face straight into my palm.

"As I was saying," Ms. Smithburg continued, oblivious to my expression of dismay, "this is a team project. Please use this class period to choose a topic. I am handing out sheets with some suggested subjects, but you are free to choose any period in American history so long as you both agree. Now, as I was also saying, I kind of hate reading term papers so I'm inviting you to think of something creative. Perhaps a PowerPoint presentation or some American history graphic novellas or—"

A voice from the back of the room called out, "Oh, oh, can we do a rap? Wiki-wiki-*what*!" A few meatheads chuckled appreciatively.

Ms. Smithburg's expression was wry. "I was just about to say that the only rule is that there will be no rap! That idea is so played and this is an AP class, so I'll be looking for something a lot more substantial. I might accept a one-act hip-hop opera if you thought you could do it without it being pathetic and embarrassing." There was a smattering of laughter as the would-be rapper was jostled by his buddies.

Ms. Smithburg handed out the last of her papers and folded her arms, but not in an authoritarian or mean way. "So, you will be graded on your command of the chosen subject matter, your creativity, and your ability to work well with your partner. This will account for fifty percent of your overall grade, so you've got your work cut out for you." She held up her hands and made playful snipping motions at us with her fingers. "I think that's everything. Any questions, come see me, but for now, get to work."

If I could have cried, I might have. Fortunately, I physically lost the ability to cry decades ago. My brother, the mad scientist, says it has to do with a lack of available fluid in my physiology and that I could probably reverse it by ingesting a simple saline solution of water and sodium iodide, or table salt. What a nerd. Plus, why the hell would I drink a glass of synthetic tears just so I could cry semi-synthetic tears? He claims it could also help with some other physical problems I have, like dry mouth and occasional muscle cramps, but I have a hard enough time keeping up with what my parents and teachers want me to do without taking orders from my ten-year-old brother.

It's funny, though—no matter how long it's been since I last cried, I still get that same stinging feeling behind my eyes.

After ten or thirty-six hard blinks, I was finally able to make myself look at this kid, Eli Matthews, who was sitting across from me with that dumb smile still on his face, waiting expectantly for me to say something. Well, he could just keep waiting. As far as I was concerned, just because someone is late due to getting his braces polished or tightened or whatever he was doing, it doesn't make us a team. I wanted to work alone, and I felt betrayed by Ms. Smithburg and angry with this kid for just being there and yes, maybe I was being irrational, but teenage vampires have mood swings too, and I was having a bad day, okay? I played the silent card.

"Hi. Eli," he said, jabbing his finger into his own chest. Oh, nice, I get paired up with the one kid in AP history who specializes in one-syllable sentences. I gave him my patented sarcastic smirk—it looks like a smile, but it's totally obvious I don't mean it.

"Matthews," he croaked. "I, um . . . It's funny. I actually . . . I think I just friended you . . . on Facebook? A few days ago?"

Yeah, right. As if he couldn't remember whether or not he'd done such a thing, because of all the thousands of friends he was communing with every day online. Of course, as soon as I thought that, I realized how ironic it was coming from me, a girl with only a pictureless profile and not one single friend. But still.

"Oh, did you? I don't go online a lot." Lie. Total lie. What else was I supposed to say, though? Eager to change the subject, I started flipping through the sheaf of papers Ms. Smithburg had handed out. "So, I guess we're stuck working together on this thing. I usually work alone, but I guess we'll just have to deal with it. What do you want to do?"

"Um, I wouldn't say—I wouldn't consider—not stuck, really. Uh . . ."

I could barely keep myself from finishing this poor kid's sentences for him. I started to feel bad for him. He must have seen the pitying look on my face. "Sorry, I'm, uh, loopy. Pain medicine from the orthodontist. Woo-hoo!"

I couldn't help laughing a little. Lucky for him he was telling *me* rather than unknowingly confessing it to one of our vampire classmates. Before he knew it, he'd be behind the gym bleachers, glamoured and tapped for a pint of blood in the name of a cheap high. Glamouring, for those of you who've never read a vampire book, is a thing we're supposed to be able to do, where we kind of put a human in a trance so that they'll do our bidding or what have you. I'm guessing it's an evolutionary trait left over from the days when vampires needed to feed directly from humans rather than getting "takeout" from a crooked phlebotomist looking to make a quick buck. Anyway, it's one of those vampire characteristics that you'd probably expect to be a myth but is actually true. I mean, I'd heard it was true, but I'd never really had the ovaries to try it before and I'd never really had a reason. Plus, Ma was always going on about how unethical it was.

Even loopy on dentist drugs, Eli Matthews didn't seem as bad as I'd originally thought. I'd seen him around a few times, but I'd never noticed how tall and broad he was, maybe because he had a real baby face. Up close, I noticed for the first time that his fair skin was covered with a constellation of cinnamon-colored freckles. He was wearing what looked like a decades-old T-shirt with a cracked and faded decal celebrating an obscure band I vaguely remembered from the eighties. I wondered whether he actually knew and liked their music or if it was just a costume for a kid who was trying to pass for cool.

Eli raised his hand like you would to get a teacher's attention. It took me a moment to realize he was waiting for me to stop staring at him and to call on him.

"What?" I said.

"I was thinking we could do . . . maybe something, like, about the Vietnam War and how . . . and how it kinda compares to the war in Iraq? And contrasts?"

God, he seemed so nervous talking to me. Was it possible that somehow, subconsciously, he sensed that I was someone he should fear? No, because then why would he have asked to be my friend online? Maybe it was because . . . *no*. It couldn't be because he liked me, could it? I instantly chastised myself for considering the possibility. I was not the kind of girl, or vampire, that boys liked. I slid my glasses up my nose and cleared my throat. Suddenly, my mouth was as dry as sand.

"I don't know very much about the Vietnam War," I lied again. I'm a very experienced liar, but all of a sudden, I hated doing it. I didn't want to look this boy in the eye and be dishonest, or play dumb, but there really wasn't anything else I could do. Truth is, I was in high school during the Vietnam War, same as I was now, and I remembered boys from the town I lived in going off to fight and not coming back. I had often thought of how unfair it was that their bravery was rewarded with premature death, while I was basically given eternal life for no better reason than the greed of some cowardly vampire. Just the idea put my stomach in knots.

"Okay, um . . . what about something else?" said Eli Matthews. "Oh, um . . . okay . . . the Cold War? With Russia?" He gestured so wildly, I think I actually laughed. Okay, I snorted.

"Jeez, you totally love subjects with the word *war* in them!"

He laughed too, and shrugged. I didn't have any better ideas myself.

"Well, it looks like chance created a great duo!" Ms. Smithburg glided toward us and leaned over our desks. "Have the two of you decided on a topic for your project yet?"

"Not exactly," Eli replied. "We've thrown . . . We've been discussing a couple ideas. Nothing has stuck, so far. So, yeah." Clearly, I wasn't the only female who made him nervous.

"Hmmm," she said. "Do you mind if I make a suggestion? I'm really good at this!" Ms. Smithburg beamed at Eli. "I see you're wearing army boots, Mr. Matthews. Was one of your ideas comparing and contrasting the Vietnam and Iraq wars?"

Eli blushed.

"Good," she said, "but maybe a little obvious, and maybe not a subject that sings to Ms. Jones." Ms. Smithburg turned her smile on me. Suddenly, my favorite teacher was making me feel kind of nervous. The hairs on the back of my neck prickled ever so slightly. What was that about?

"She's a deep girl, Mr. Matthews," said Ms. Smithburg. "Lotta thoughts going on in that head of hers. I'm thinking something post-1929, after the stock-market crash. When I look at this girl, the first thing that comes to mind is the 'Dirty Thirties.' When I look at her, I think 'Dust Bowl.' Shall I put the two of you down for that?" Without waiting for an answer from either of us, she made a quick note in her lesson plan book, then rapped her knuckles sharply on my desk for emphasis. She swept off, leaving me with my mouth agape and three words running through my head: *What the fu—*

"Fun!" Eli crowed. "I totally never would have thought of that, but it seems like it would be fun to do."

I couldn't believe what I was hearing. He thought

it would be *fun*? If only he had one-millionth of one per-cent of an idea just how unfun it was. But how could he be expected to know—he hadn't lived it.

Also, out of every possible event in the history of American history, how had Ms. Smithburg just happened to pull that one out of thin air? I know vampires are gen-erally the ones going around scaring everybody, but for once, I was fully freaked out. I proved that to myself when the end-of-period bell rang and startled me so much, I thought my heart was going to start again!

Eli Matthews was grabbing his things, getting ready to go to his next class, but I couldn't make myself move. "I can tell you're still not sure, but this will be good. No, *great*. I'll see you. I'll see you at lunch! Cafeteria!"

I wasn't sure what to think. I wasn't sure how to feel about this guy. I wasn't sure if this project was a good idea. Also, I wasn't sure exactly where the cafeteria was or if I could bring myself to show up there for the midday meal known to mortals as "lunch."

# four

**I clutched my books to my chest nervously as I entered the Port Lincoln High School cafeteria for the first time since I'd enrolled.** The benefit to being turned into a vampire before your boobs grow is that if you want to clutch anything to your chest, you can really get a tight seal between your front and whatever it is you're clutching.

I was worried that it would be one of those situations where I'd wander around looking for a seat while kids sneered at me and put their bags down on empty chairs, but I found a table right off the bat. Granted, I looked like a total pariah sitting alone at a table for eight people, but I had a long history of taking what I could get. Despite deciding that this Eli kid was semi-okay, I was here against my better judgment. I wasn't even sure if he'd remember to meet me, but I certainly wasn't going to wander around looking for him. I had my minimal dignity. I opened up one of my books and pretended I was reading.

"Such a bookworm!" Timothy Hunt slid into the seat next to me. "What are you reading?"

I was caught off guard, and Timothy's dazzling smile didn't do much to help me recover. "It's . . . um, about . . ." Busted, I had to look at the book's jacket. "It's women's lit." Would I ever stop looking like an idiot around this guy?

Timothy peered at the page I was open to. He grunted thoughtfully. "Ah, Virginia Woolf. I knew her."

"Oh, yeah?" Then I remembered who—and what— I was talking to. "Wait, do you mean you *knew her* knew her? Like, when she was alive?"

Timothy laughed. "No, no. I mean I knew her work at one time. You're not the only one of us who was ever interested in anything, you know."

I was slightly embarrassed. Obviously, my secretly superior attitude wasn't quite as secret as I thought it was. But still, why were high-school vampires such slackers? I decided to ask him as gently as possible. "Too bad you didn't *know her* know her. She might still be alive now! Ha-ha. So, why are high-school vampires such slackers?"

Timothy laughed huskily but glanced around to make sure nobody heard me before his iridescent and breathtaking eyes locked on to mine. "You're quite young, no? How long has it been for you? Perhaps ninety or a hundred years?"

It wasn't even that long.

"I was like you once," he said gently. "Maybe not as bright, but I studied and read. But a lot has happened in the past few centuries. More great works of art and literature than anyone could ever absorb. Not to mention all the wonderful television shows that just keep coming. My TiVo is about to burst!"

I smiled. He was obviously trying to put me at ease.

"Between computers and scientific discoveries, it gets to be almost too much just to function every day without going looking for extra things to think about." He shrugged and leaned back in his chair. He wasn't particularly tall and his build was trim, but there was something about him, his mannerisms, that was so mature and confident. The more I looked at him, the more I found myself wanting to look at him. "I'm okay with being just your average high-school fellow," he continued. "It's not like I'm going to MIT in two years or anything."

I felt a little ashamed. I hadn't thought of it that way until he explained it. I couldn't really ever see myself thinking that way, but lately I couldn't really picture myself sticking with the vampire thing for the next two centuries either. I wasn't sure if that article I'd been poring over all weekend was true, but I was electrified by the possibility that there might someday be a cure for vampirism. Granted, being a blood-intolerant vampire—and honestly, a geek—was a total drag and I was over it, but I had to think that even someone like Timothy, who seemed like he was so cool and together, might change his circumstances if he could.

As if he'd read my mind, Timothy said, "I'm sorry to be dour. I'm just tired, that's all." His handsome smile changed just then. It was still a smile, but the kind of smile an adult puts on when a friend has gotten a promotion *he* was hoping for. It was a smile he didn't look old enough to be wearing. I felt a phantom ache in my useless heart. Impulsively, I reached into my notebook and retrieved the folded printout I had stashed there.

"Have you seen this?" I handed the story to Timothy and watched closely for his reaction. As his eyes moved across the headline, his brow furrowed and he had a sharp intake of breath. Before he could utter a word, we were joined by a most unwelcome guest.

"Again? You two are making quite a habit out of these little one-on-one tête-à-têtes." Astrid pulled a chair out for herself, loudly scraping it across the cafeteria linoleum. Vampires are good at sneaking up on humans, but usually one vampire will notice another one coming. Unless that one vampire is totally distracted by a third vampire's insanely gorgeous eyes. In any case, I was getting sick of Astrid's habit of interrupting us.

"You two on a lunch date is sort of absurd, no? If you're not careful, everyone will think something's going on between the two of you, Tim." She looked at him, then at me. "Or maybe you'd like everyone to think that . . . *Jane.*"

Timothy discreetly folded the tattered printer paper I'd given him and slipped it into the pocket of his vintage wool jacket. "Astrid, won't you please sit down with us? Jane and I were just discussing . . . Virginia Woolf." Astrid stared, so he added: "She's a famous writer."

"I know who Virginia Woolf is, I just don't give a shit," Astrid snapped. She looked back and forth between Timothy and me. "Do *you*? Really? Give a shit?"

I was trying to think of an awesomely witty rejoinder that would make Timothy chuckle wryly while taking Astrid down ten pegs, when out of the corner of my eye I saw the lumbering frame of Eli Matthews heading toward us. He arrived, out of breath.

"Jane. Sorry I'm late. I had to stay after class because I got a problem wrong on my calculus quiz and I had to show Mr. Kirchner that, actually, he was mistaken and I had . . ." He noticed, a little late, that I wasn't the only one sitting there, and ended his story abruptly. "He, um, changed my grade."

It was interesting to watch Eli, self-conscious to begin

with, become even more self-conscious as he realized he was relaying a tale of grade grubbing in front of complete strangers. He stuck out his broad, freckled hand to Timothy. "Uh, I'm Eli. Hi." Timothy accepted his hand graciously. I half expected something to happen when they made contact, but Eli's face didn't show any change. Timothy was obviously very skilled at controlling his supernatural energy. Was there anything he couldn't do?

"Oh," I said, realizing it was rude of me not to make introductions. "Timothy Hunt, this is Eli Matthews from my American history class." They shook hands and nodded, an imitation of a gesture between grown men.

"That's Astrid," I said.

Eli offered his hand halfway to Astrid before her pinched smile and glaring eyes made it clear that she wasn't the type who dabbled in niceties. Still, Eli tried to save face by turning his aborted shake into a timid wave. I felt a pang of pity.

"Uh, sit," I said. I was cordial to Eli, but I didn't want to give anyone the impression that we were besties. That was probably mean, but I was pretty new to this talking-to-others thing, and I was trying to navigate carefully. I turned to Timothy. "Eli and I are working on an assignment together this term. We're not really sure what we're doing yet."

"But I . . . um . . . was thinking about what Ms. Smith-burg assigned us." Eli unzipped his hulking backpack and pulled out a thick stack of library books, letting them thump down on the table. "So, about the Dust Bowl thing? I think she was on to something." I sort of had the gut feeling she was on to something too, but I wasn't sure what. I told my gut it was being ridiculous and to shut up.

Eli handed the top book to me and I gazed down at it. A sepia-toned photograph of a dirty farmer looked back at me, sending a shiver down my spine. I bit my lip.

"I thought maybe we could do some"—Eli swallowed—"do a little work over lunch?"

I'll be the first to admit that I am socially awkward, mostly because of the fact that up until three days ago, it had been ages since I was social with anyone except my socially awkward family, but even I could tell this was weird. Astrid scoffed as Eli rummaged through his back-pack and emerged with a crinkled brown bag. If he noticed her noise, he didn't show it.

"Please, you two go ahead," said Astrid. "Tim and I need to go do some work on a project of our own for biology. We're studying the circulatory system!" She secretly flashed me a tiny little bit of fang to illustrate her tiny lit-tle inside joke, then grabbed Timothy's arm to signal that he would be leaving with her. Timothy looked at me and rolled his sapphire eyes but didn't protest. As they stood and passed Eli, Astrid patted his arm in a gesture of exaggerated kindness that crossed the border right into mocking.

"And, Eli," she said, "please look out for our Jane. She just admitted to us that she hasn't eaten a thing since Friday night! We worry about her!"

Eli nodded moronically and smiled as Astrid swept out of the cafeteria with Timothy by her side. I scanned his eyes to try to see if she'd put a little whammy on him, but I couldn't tell. "She seems nice," Eli said. He really was clueless. "So, are you gonna . . . Do you want me to wait . . . while you get lunch? Or something?"

I didn't know what to say. I considered telling him that Astrid was a sociopath, or that I was fasting for religious reasons. But then I wondered if he'd ask what religion I was. Would I be able to keep up some charade religion for an entire term? It was obvious that I had to lie, but I decided it was better to go with something simple.

"I ran out of the house without my lunch money," I said, "so I'm just going to wait and have something after school."

I spastically grabbed the top Dust Bowl book and started paging through it in an effort to move on—when suddenly, half a tuna sandwich was shoved under my nose.

"You gotta eat, right?" said Eli. "You like tuna? Brain food, my, um . . . my mom says." Eli seemed to realize, for once, that what he'd just said might not have been the coolest thing in the world. His freckled neck flushed, but to his credit, he smiled. "I know you're probably dying to hear what else my mom says, but you're gonna have to eat this sandwich first."

He held the sandwich out to me. I didn't have the energy to make up another lie about being vegetarian. He no doubt had an apple or carrot sticks in his bag anyway. He was being friendly and I wanted to let him.

I took the sandwich.

It had been so long since I'd actually held regular food in my hand. Even before I'd become a vampire, food was something that had become scarce and unfamiliar, and since then, I hadn't really had much excuse to think about it.

Still, sometimes I *did* think about it. Mostly when I saw television commercials for tiny frozen dinners that were supposed to make people thin, or yogurt in tubes that was supposed to give kids energy. It all seemed kind of dumb to me. If you could eat, why not do it right? Why not use the professional knives on your granite countertop to chop some fresh vegetables to simmer on your six-burner stove? Why not peel and slice a single perfect aromatic and sweet orange or shell some salted peanuts, if you could?

I felt my fingertips sinking into the moist wheat bread. I couldn't just sit there holding it. While Eli was looking down at another of his Dust Bowl books, I surreptitiously sniffed at the filling. Vampires have a good sense of smell. In fact, it's so good that the whole world sort of smells like a mixture of all the aromas surrounding us. So we've become adept at zeroing in on particular scents while ignoring others. You could say we're almost like bloodhounds. For the most part, we're able to block out the smell of food because it's useless to us. I say "for the most part" because we really do hate garlic, but only because the strong smell is so hard to ignore. That's why not many pizza lovers fall prey to random crazed vamp attacks. But I had been turning my nose up at food for so long now that I was the tiniest bit curious, so I inhaled.

And oh, God.

It was not good. Not good at all.

My father never complained about his job at the plant, but I recognized that it was kind of unusual for a man who doesn't eat to spend night after night producing snack foods for people who never seem to stop eating. I also knew that when he came home in the morning, his clothes gave off a faint odor of something I didn't love, the way I imagine an auto mechanic might smell a little motor-oily to his family. But I had no idea just how rank and vile food could smell when you took a great big whiff of it on purpose. I made a mental note to thank my father for his sacrifice as I blinked my stinging eyes. When Eli looked up at me expectantly, I panicked.

"It's got celery in it," he said. "My mom—I mean, the lady who makes my lunch," he deadpanned, "she always puts that in there. It's good."

At that moment, I realized that if I didn't do something, he was just going to keep talking about the damn sandwich his mother made and asking me questions and looking at me. I'm positive my eyes were as wide as saucers as I took a deep breath and bit into the soggy bread. Satisfied, Eli went back to scanning the book in front of him. I think he started talking again about what a great idea Ms. Smithburg had, but I was no longer listening.

Once, when I was very small, we'd traded some of the wheat my father managed to grow for some fresh eggs, which my mother cooked for us. Even though I'd been famished, when I bit into a little piece of shell, I wasn't able to eat any more. You know what I'm talking about. Or maybe at some point you've found a hair in your food? Well, imagine a similar feeling, but rather than a shell it's a little beak and instead of just hair, it's hair with dandruff stuck to it and still attached to a piece of human scalp. Either of those scenarios would be a little more pleasant than how I felt with this small piece of sandwich in my mouth. Every chew triggered the same refrain inside my head: *This is wrong! This is wrong! This is wrong! This is wrong!*

The lunch bell interrupted the ringing in my ears.

"So, are you on board?" I heard Eli ask. My cheeks were lined with sticky tuna sandwich pulp, which was apparently poison to me. I had to answer, and in order to answer, I had to swallow. It was excruciatingly foul. If there was any way my white skin could have gone paler, I'm sure it had.

"Whatever you think," I croaked. "I gotta go."

I snatched my books and sprinted out of the cafeteria, flinging the remainder of the sandwich in a garbage can outside the door. I made it down the hall in time to bang through the girls'-room door and into the nearest stall. On my knees, I leaned over the toilet and heaved. Repeatedly. The sandwich I'd swallowed was long gone, but it was obvious that my body was trying to teach me a very important lesson about experimenting with people food. When it was over, I leaned my cool cheek against the metal wall, which felt warm by comparison. I grabbed a wad of toilet paper, wiped my mouth, and stood up. I was considering my chances of sneaking into my last-period geometry class late when I stepped out of the stall and saw Mrs. Rosebush, the assistant principal, leaning against the sinks. She was evidently waiting for me.

Her long, wavy brown hair was threaded with silvery gray and tied up in a loose knot. Her clothes were just as loose and long. In all my years in schools, I'd seen her type time and time again, even before there was a word for it: the aging hippie, devoting her life to Nurturing Young Minds. I didn't know for sure, but I guessed she drove some type of Volkswagen. She clearly wanted to "rap."

"It's Jane, right?"

I nodded, not sure I was able to speak normally just yet.

"Are you feeling all right, Jane?" She stepped closer to me, presumably to touch my forehead for any sign of fever, but maybe to see if I reeked of booze. I ducked her hand and backed away.

"I'm okay," I said. "I just ate something that didn't agree with me, but I'm fine now. I'm late for geometry."

"I think if you're ill, you shouldn't go to class. I think you need to see the nurse."

Uh, the *last* thing I needed was to see the nurse, because the *last* thing I needed to do today was have someone take my temperature and then watch her eyes pop out when it was 26.6 degrees lower than normal. I'd had it happen thirty-something years ago, and that time I convinced the woman her thermometer was broken. But right now, I just didn't feel up to it.

"Seriously, I'm fine. I swear. I mean, it's incredibly tempting to get out of geometry—who wouldn't want that? But I'm not sick, so it wouldn't be right. I *want* to go to geometry. That's how fine I am." I realized I was blathering and abruptly shut up.

I got lucky. Mrs. Rosebush was the kind of educator who liked to believe that she was developing a special relationship with every kid who passed through her halls. She thought she understood me better than any other teacher here ever could.

She had no idea.

"Well, if you won't go to the nurse, I want you to go to the library and read quietly until the end of the day. I'll give you a pass." She took a pink pad of hallway passes out of the pocket of her long duster and scrawled on one before tearing it off and handing it to me. She raised her eyebrows and gave me a little smile as I took it.

"Jane, I know you're new in town and being in a new place isn't easy. But this is a good place. We take care of each other here. So, I'm around if you ever need to talk. Okay?"

I figured I needed to play along if I was ever going to get out of there. I looked down at the tile floor.

"Okay. Thanks." I managed a small, grateful, fake-yet-convincing smile as I turned and left the bathroom.

I headed toward the library, fully intending to do as I had been told. Then I realized: if I just held on to my pass and said I'd forgotten to turn it in, I probably wouldn't get into any trouble. If anybody even asked at all. I decided my day had already been long enough. I tucked the pass into my notebook, and when I reached the library, I just walked past the door and out the north exit of the school. The air, I noticed, was colder than I was.

# $five$

**"Honey, I'm home!" I yelled as I banged through the back door of my house into the empty kitchen.** When you're a teen vampire stuck in a suburban wasteland, it's the little things like being a smart-⬤ that really keep you going.

My mother appeared in the doorway, finger to her lips. "Jane, your father is sleeping!" she hissed. "What are you doing home? I thought you were spending the last period of school reading quietly in the library."

I get it that mothers come equipped with some kind of sixth sense that tingles when something is up with their offspring, but this was a little ridiculous. Had decades of mom experience allowed her to actually start reading my thoughts? "How did you—"

"Mrs. Rosebush from the school called."

"Oh, God . . ."

"She said she was concerned because she heard you

vomiting in the bathroom after lunch. I'm sure there must be some kind of mistake."

"No, I was in the bathroom. And there was puke."

"Jane, those kids didn't goad you into drinking blood again, did they?"

Logically, due to my being conscious, my mother must have known that wasn't the case, but why not take an already embarrassing situation and compound it by bringing up another recently embarrassing situation, right?

"No, Ma. They didn't."

"Then why on earth were you sick?"

I knew she wasn't going to drop it until I gave her an answer, yet I still tried to avoid it. "It's a long story, Ma."

She folded her arms. "Well, I've got all the time in eternity to hear it, so go ahead."

I sighed heavily. Scientists theorize that people sigh when they have low oxygen levels in their bodies. I theorize that teenagers, both human and vampire alike, have low oxygen in their bodies due to parental smothering.

"I took a bite of a sandwich and I threw up. That's it."

"A sandwich? Jane, you see your father come home from work feeling sick just from the smell of human food. What would possess you to take a bite of a sandwich?"

I had been trying to keep my voice low so I wouldn't wake my father, but frustration overwhelmed me. I said, louder than I should have, "*Ma!* I was working on a project with a boy over lunch. Just like you're always pushing me to do. He's a regular boy who brought a sandwich from home, made by *his* pushy mother. When he noticed I wasn't eating anything, he pushily insisted that I share it. He wouldn't drop it, so I had to take a bite. End of story!"

Her face softened a bit, almost imperceptibly. She resumed speaking in a low tone.

"I'm just very concerned. I know you're almost a century old and it seems like you've been through everything. But because of who you are, and what you are, you still think like a child thinks—an intelligent and gifted girl, but still just a girl nonetheless. It worries me that you could be so easily pushed into doing things that you know will be bad for you."

I didn't raise my voice again. There was no need to shout what I was about to say. "Well, you know what, Ma? It worries me that you can't see the truth of the situation I'm in. You don't want me to be pushed into anything unless it's you doing the pushing. You want to have absolute control over my life and you're constantly telling me what I should and shouldn't do, *but* it's the very things you tell me I should be doing that are getting me into trouble. Sometimes I wish you weren't in my life at all."

The instant I said it, I wanted to take it back. I assumed

that my words would reignite her anger, but the way her forehead crinkled and her eyes fluttered, I could tell she was feeling the sting of phantom tears that probably couldn't appear so many hours after she'd fed. She knew I was telling the truth. I may not have used my fangs to draw blood, but my mouth could be dangerous in other ways.

"Ma, I know you worry. But you don't need to. I'm basically unkillable except for a couple very unlikely scenarios, right? So any mistake I make is just a mistake. Unless it involves accidentally walking into a track-and-field practice and getting javelined through the chest, I'll be okay."

"You're right, Jo." She cringed at her little slip of the tongue. "I meant to say 'Jane.' I could stand to trust you more and to give you more space than I have been." Now it was her turn to sigh. "Unfortunately, your vice principal wants to have a meeting with your father and me about this vomiting incident."

"A meeting? Why?"

"Well, she didn't want to alarm me, but she's convinced that you're displaying the classic symptoms of a teenage girl with an eating disorder."

Oh, crap. Of course. A touchy-feely former guidance counselor eavesdrops on a ninety-two-pound, pale sophomore retching in a stall after lunch and what else is she supposed to think? Her extensive experience with adolescents would no doubt lead her to one obvious conclusion. If Mrs. Rosebush only had an inkling of what she'd actually stumbled upon, she might have sped off in her earthy-crunchy mobile and never looked back.

"What did you tell her?"

"What *could* I tell her? I said we would come in tomorrow. She wants you to be there too."

"Oh, that'll be lots of fun. I'm sure she'll have a team of doctors ready to whisk me away to a treatment facility."

"Jane, stop. This isn't one of those depressing reality shows. But we do have to think of something we can tell her that will get this idea that you have an eating disorder out of her mind."

"Oh, I know! Let's tell her I was hurling because I'm pregnant! That will totally distract her from my bulimia."

"Jane, that's not even funny." Even as she tried to frown, the corners of her mouth turned up involuntarily. It was at least a little funny. After all, I was in my nineties and still a total virgin. Not to mention the fact that vampires tend to reproduce in a we-bite-you-then-feed-you-our-blood kind of way, rather than in the mainstream sex-resulting-in-a-cuddly-baby way that humans seem to favor. There were times when I'd been overcome by sadness at the idea that I would never be a mother myself, but I've gotten used to it. And right now, the mental image of my own mother telling Mrs. Rosebush that I was with child was absolutely hilarious to me. Ma's snorting told me that she agreed.

Our moment of shared laughter was interrupted by knocking at the front door. My mother and I stared at each other for a second. Visitors to our household were a rarity, and even though she possessed the strength and ability to overpower any intruder, after all these years Ma was still understandably paranoid about inviting anyone into our home. Ever. Still, it wouldn't do to let whomever it was just stand there, lest he start ringing the doorbell, which could wake my father.

We held hands as we walked from the kitchen into the living room. I patted my mother's arm before taking a deep breath and opening the door just a crack. Standing there, fist poised to rap on the wood again, was Eli Matthews, with an old wooden skateboard under his arm. Relieved but exasperated, I opened the door all the way.

"What are you doing here?" I asked, perhaps a bit too rudely.

He answered in what I now knew was his usual way— a rapid tumble of words: "I waited for you after geometry, to see if you wanted to walk home together . . . y'know, so we could talk about our project on the way. But when you didn't come out, I tried to catch you at your locker.

Obviously, as you know, I didn't. But I caught up with that girl Astrid and her friend—Celeste, I think? I asked if they had seen you around. Astrid said no but that she thought you'd be psyched if I just dropped by. I asked if they knew where you lived and they didn't exactly, but then they actually went to the office and somehow got the secretary to give them your home address, which I thought was pretty unorthodox. But anyway, I figured since you all are good friends and they said you'd be cool . . . I'd just come over. I hope that's . . . I hope you don't mind." Eli finally stopped to breathe. I realized I'd been holding my breath too, waiting for him to finish. Noticing my mother standing beside me, he stuck out his hand. "Hi, Mrs. Jones. I'm Eli Matthews."

Ma slid me a sideways glance before accepting Eli's hand. It looked as if she were simultaneously baffled and charmed by this goofy kid. I was simultaneously thinking that she was crazy and he was a crazy stalker.

"Ma, this is the guy I was telling you about. We're doing the project together. For American history?"

"Really? You told your mom about me? That's . . . wow. I mean, it's not a big, big deal, but it's nice. Nice to meet you, by the way, ma'am."

"Nice to meet you too, Eli." My mother smiled and squinted her eyes against the autumn sun coming through the open door. She looked behind her into our empty, undisturbed living room, then back at Eli before saying, "Please forgive me. Would you like to come in?"

Before I could stop him or say a word, that tall, baby-faced, befreckled kid had dropped his board on our front steps and shouldered his way into our home. I looked from his metallic grin to Ma's frozen smile. It was hard to tell which one of us was the most awkward.

"Uh, can I offer you anything?" my mother said. I elbowed her sharply in the side to shut her up. "Of course, I haven't been grocery shopping this week, so perhaps a drink . . . of water? Perhaps?"

Real smooth, Ma.

"Oh, no thanks, Mrs. Jones. I had some water earlier today. I like to stay hydrated. Thank you, though. I really just came by to see if Jane wanted to brainstorm for a while on our history project. It counts for a huge part of our grade, and I think the earlier we—"

"I can't. Sorry. Can't do it right now," I said. I didn't owe him an explanation, but the way his grin dimmed a little made me feel like I should give one anyway. Even if it had to be another fib. "I can't because . . . we're going shopping. Me and my mother." I widened my eyes at Ma until she caught on and nodded slightly in agreement.

"Oh, okay. Well, then." His smile vanished completely, and I almost felt bad for him. Then, just as quickly, he brightened. "Wait, are you going grocery shopping now? Because I could come with you and we could talk in the car a little bit before we got there and then . . ."

"Nope. Not grocery shopping. We need to get some . . ." I struggled to come up with something that would prevent Eli from reinviting himself on our bogus excursion. "We need to get some . . . girl stuff." Girl stuff? Good one.

My mother unhelpfully jumped in. "Yeah. We're going bra shopping. They're on sale today."

While I was looking at my mother aghast, I noticed Eli, glancing at my chest. I turned to him and his eyes snapped back up to my face.

"Really?" he said. "I mean, of course. You don't need me tagging along for that. You've got to focus on . . . that."

Sometimes, when your mother utterly humiliates you by calling a classmate's attention to your bust, the only thing you can do is own it. "Yup," I said. "A bra sale can be really competitive. Gotta get our game faces on." Originally, my intent was to get rid of Eli quickly, but as I noticed how much redder each additional mention of the word *bra* made his face, it was tempting to keep him around for a few minutes just to mess with him. Then Ma ruined it by taking pity on him.

"Eli, we should be back before too long. Why don't you come by after you eat dinner tonight and you and Jane can work on your project for a couple of hours then?" I could not believe she was doing this to me.

"Really? That would be great. Thank you, Mrs. Jones. So, Jane, I guess I'll see you around seven?"

Before I could even think of another excuse, he was out the door and on his skateboard, pushing down our front walk. I watched him shift his weight to turn the corner and roll off down our street. "I guess," I said to nobody, shoving the door closed. Then I wheeled around, ready to pounce on my meddlesome mother—but she was already at the front closet, wearing an old L.L.Bean barn jacket and sunglasses, trying to dig the keys to the Volvo out of her overstuffed purse.

"What are you doing?"

"Well, I guess we're going shopping, right?"

"Ma!" I rolled my eyes. "There isn't really a bra sale! *You* made it up, remember? I was just trying to blow him off."

"Jane, I know. But now he's coming over at seven and we really do have to pick up a few things so this house looks a little more . . . lived in." She looked at me, on-the-ball mother to clueless teenaged daughter. "I'd like to be able to show your guest a little hospitality."

I wanted to say, *You seem to be forgetting that it was*

*hospitality that got us into this whole mess all those years ago.* But I had used my mouth for evil enough for one day. In a weird way, my mother even looked kind of excited as she rummaged around in the bottom of her bag and came up with a fistful of keys. So, for once, I just shut up.

# Six

**The next morning, I stayed in bed later than usual.** My atrophied stomach muscles ached. Apparently, vomiting is more of an abdominal workout than I'd remembered. "Jaaaa-aaane. Time to get up, Sleeping Doody!" I opened one eye to see my little brother poking his head between the heavy velveteen light-blocking drapes on my canopy bed.

"Ugh, Zachary," I said, calling him by the new alias he'd chosen when we'd moved to this town. "Can you never come in my room without knocking again?"

He banged his knuckles on the wall above my head. "I'm knocking! Is this good?" I grabbed a throw pillow and threw it at his head. (That's what they're for, right?) Zachary dodged, then darted out of my room, shouting, "Ma, Jane is throwing things at me!" I knew it was pointless to wish that the twerp would grow up, but I couldn't help myself.

Slowly, I sat up and eased my legs over the side of the bed, gingerly placing my feet on the floor. I am not a morning vampire. I mean, most vampires don't exactly jump out of bed whistling a tune when the sun comes up, but even before I was a vampire, I hated mornings. Even when I was just a girl, living in a little house on the prairie, getting me up and out of bed to do my chores was like pulling teeth. And speaking of teeth, my fangs were out. I was hungry and weak.

I shuffled across my bedroom carpet and switched off the humming sunlamps before my skin started to sizzle. One really small good thing about being a vampire is that you rarely sweat, so BO is not much of a problem. Bathing wasn't something we did super-regularly back in the day, and even though I like to have a soak sometimes at night to relax, I can definitely skip a shower in the morning with no problem. I didn't even bother sniffing my armpits. I felt around for my glasses, poked myself in the eye twice trying to get them on my face, then pulled on some "vintage" jeans, which I'd actually bought new in the nineties, and a gray hoodie from the athletic department of some school I'd gone to ten or twelve years ago.

Contrary to what you'd think, I don't go around wearing Gothy capes or black lipstick. Any dark clothes or makeup would just accentuate how pale my complexion is, and that's not really what I'm going for. Sure, I'd love to wear something a little more girly or trendy, but I have fewer curves than the letter *I*. Plus, I would never ask for the money. My father breaks his back making crackers just to earn enough to pay the rent and our insane electric bills here.

As I reached the top of the stairs to make my slow descent, I heard my dad coming in the back door, after his shift at the plant. I made my way to the kitchen in time to see him, so tired, ruffle Zach's hair and smooch Ma on the forehead. When he saw me, he looked up and winked before taking a seat. Just like a normal family you'd see on a TV show, but instead of passing buttered toast, my mother was setting defrosted black-market blood-bank donations in tiny half-full shot glasses at everyone's place. Except for in front of me. What I got was a teaspoon containing what looked to be about two drops of the incredibly rare Bombay blood. It was twice my normal portion.

"Jane, I thought it would be a good idea if you fed a little more this morning . . . after everything yesterday." My mother spoke in that tone a person uses when they want to sound like something isn't a big deal, but actually they think it's a really huge deal.

"Everything yesterday?" Dad asked. "What happened yesterday?"

"Oh, nothing serious. Jane got a little sick at school."
Ma shrugged.

"Janie-girl, are you okay?" No matter what year it
was or what alias I was using, my dad would always tack an
"—ie dash girl" on the end. I secretly loved it.

"I'm fine, Dad, really. We should all just forget all
about it."

"Actually, Jim, Jane's vice principal has asked us to
come in for a meeting about it today. She's under the impression that Jane might have an eating disorder. . . ."

"Your vice principal thinks you have an eating disorder?" howled Zachary. "That's a good one! She has no idea
that it would be metabolically impossible for *you* to
attempt to eat anything without spewing everywhere,
whether you want to or not!" My brother cackled and
sniffed at his glass.

"Zachary, that's enough," my dad said. "Drink your
breakfast."

"What about Jane? Shouldn't she have her breakfast before it turns into a tiny scab?" Zachary's face grew thoughtful. "Actually, that would make an interesting experiment.
Do scabs contain any nutrients beneficial to vampires? I
could conduct a trial—"

"Zach! Eat." My father was a man of few words, but my
brother knew it was time to shut his fang hole. He sullenly

downed his glass. I couldn't stay mad at him. As tough as it was for me to be stuck at sixteen, I imagined it was even more difficult to be eighty-five going on ten. He would be a genius by any college's standards, yet he was fated to repeat fifth grade and middle school for eternity, without ever growing an inch. If he had anything going for him socially it was that he hadn't had to deal with very many vampires his own age over the years. It seemed that all but the most unscrupulous of our kind considered it too cruel and unusual to turn a child. So he was a know-it-all and a loner and it didn't exactly make him Mr. Popular. If anyone could understand my baby brother, it was me, and I loved the kid.

"Jane, please forgive me," Zach said sweetly. Then his face split into a wicked grin. "I've completely forgotten to ask how your date went last night!"

Did I say I loved the kid? I may have misspoken. I caught myself wishing he were mortal just so I could kill him again.

"Date? What date?" My poor, confused father's head swiveled around the table looking for a clue.

"It wasn't a date, Dad. I'm doing a project with some kid and he came over to work on it last night after you left for your shift."

"Some kid? A kid from the vampire community or a *kid* kid?"

"He's a non-sucker, Dad," Zach offered. "Pasty and weird, but non-vampire nonetheless."

"I don't know if I like the idea of a stranger coming into our house while I'm not here, Dottie. It isn't safe." My brother and I exchanged a brief look, before casting our eyes elsewhere. Neither of us would ever say it, but we both thought the same thing. My father had been in the house when the worst thing possible had happened to us. So had my mother. They had both been powerless to protect us then, hadn't they? To worry about inviting some random kid into our home now seemed sort of ridiculous. Especially since any one of us probably could have glamoured him, and my mother or Zach could have easily drained him if he'd turned out to be an enemy. Picturing Eli Matthews white and wasted on my kitchen floor sent a shiver up my neck, and I shook my head to dislodge the image.

"He's a good boy, Jim. *I* invited him to come. It's good for Jane to be with children her own . . . her own age. Well, of course they're not technically the same age, but . . . you know what I mean. Anyway, it's required. We don't really have a choice." She patted my arm solicitously and my skin tingled pleasantly the way it does when one vampire touches another in a gentle way.

"Well," my father said, still looking unconvinced, "I don't like it, but I guess we can't go bucking the system.

What's the project, Janie?" My dad's face transformed from a mask of worry to the face of love as he beamed at me warmly. No matter how stiff and cold my heart, it always swelled when my father looked at me like that. But even though I was a daddy's girl all the way, I wasn't really ready to discuss my history project or my history project partner with anyone just now.

"It's no big deal, Dad. Just a history paper. But," I said, shoving my spoon into my mouth and withdrawing it with a lipsmacking *pop*, "I really have to run or I'm going to be late."

"Can I give you a ride, Magpie?" Magpie was another name he'd called me for as long as I could remember, even after I had gotten too old. Although I wasn't fond of being treated like an eternal child, it comforted me to think that I would always be my father's Magpie.

"Thanks, Daddy, but I'm going to walk. I don't want to waste any of this post-feed energy. Thank you for the breakfast, Ma." I stood up from the table, kissed my father on the cheek, and slung my backpack over my shoulders while crossing to the door.

Rather than discouraging me from walking (shock) my mother began to run through her regular checklist of questions that always preceded any time spent outdoors during daylight hours. "Are you wearing sunblock?"

"I put some on before I went to sleep." I was lying. I hadn't. I just didn't feel like getting all goopy and it was only a short way to school. Besides, aren't teenagers known for sometimes making bad choices? It was kind of my duty.

"Do you have your cell phone? In case—"

"In case I suffer a massive SPF failure during the ten-minute walk?" I cut her off. "Check."

Undeterred, she pressed on. "Are you planning on wearing a hat?"

"Ma, I'm not planning to wear a hat because I don't really have a hat face. I'll just let my hair hang in my eyes like you hate. I'll be fine." My hand on the doorknob, I thought I'd be able to make my escape, but this morning my mother had a new addition to her list.

"Don't forget—we'll see you later for that meeting with your vice principal," she reminded me.

Ugh, I *had* forgotten, momentarily, but I wasn't about to let her know that. "How could I forget?" I replied, and banged through the screen door, then bounded down the steps. It was really incredible how even just two tiny drops of blood warmed my skin against the brisk breeze. I felt more like myself than I had in weeks and I felt ready to face the day. Let Astrid torment me. Let Mrs. Rosebush pigeonhole me as a troubled teen. Let Charlotte Smithburg continue her transformation from my favorite teacher into someone who kind of freaked me out a little. And Eli Matthews? Let him be all enthusiastic and polite. Let him keep making stupid jokes and laughing at *my* stupid jokes and staring at me when he thinks I'm not looking at him.

I had caught him staring a lot during our study date the night before. No, not a date. Appointment. It was a study appointment. But Eli sure acted like he wished it had been a date. He arrived at seven o'clock on the dot, and he was wearing a clean button-down shirt and some of that body spray that's supposed to make women throw themselves at guys and tear their clothes off. It smelled like medicated dog shampoo. Luckily, I was able to tune that out because of his real scent, which reminded me the slightest bit of these cinnamon-clove cookies I remember Ma making at Christmas when I was very little and we still had plenty of food to eat. Not enough to be overpowering or sickening— just enough to make me remember, when I leaned close to him accidentally and took a big enough whiff. Ma let us work in my room, which was fine, except for when Eli flicked on my incredibly bright sleeping-lights. I made some dumb excuse about the high-wattage bulbs being there since we moved in and how I've been bugging my dad to change them. The only other light I had was a dim little desk lamp, which I snapped on instead. Thinking about it now, I realize that between the low light and the way I tried to casually throw open the drapes on my bed, it might have looked like I was trying to set some kind of mood. Ridiculous.

Ma was ridiculous too. She made a tray with some cheese we'd bought and some free crackers my dad had brought home from the plant that had been stashed in an otherwise empty cabinet. She cut vegetables into little sticks and poured cola into a glass for Eli. I had to say, "Ma, it's not a cocktail party," to get rid of her, but before she left he said, "Really, Mrs. Jones, thank you for the snacks. Truly. They look great," and grinned so wide his top and bottom braces showed. I think he really did like the food too, or he was a nervous eater, judging from the amount of crackers and crudités he put away.

I mean, it's possible he was nervous because it's possible he kind of liked me. I think that was kind of safe to assume, although I know it's bad to make assumptions. I mean, maybe the way I kept refusing to eat anything at all caused him to assume that I was too nervous to eat. And that wasn't the case. I mean, I *was* too nervous to eat, but not because of him. I was too nervous to eat because of how I'd violently regurgitated human food once already that day.

Besides, all I was really interested in was getting this

project over with. Eli seemed to like Ms. Smithburg as much as I thought I did before recent events had me questioning her intentions. He had taken her Dust Bowl idea to heart and had obviously been thinking a lot about how we could make it our own. His idea was that we could create a kind of fictional video diary of a kid our age who was living on a Midwestern farm in the mid-thirties. He suggested that we write the script together, and that he work the camera, while I did the acting. "Then I can edit the whole thing on my laptop," he said. "Add some old folk music and title cards. It'll have tons of pizzazz!"

"Pizzazz? Did you really just say 'pizzazz' on purpose?" I was teasing him, but I felt like a ball of ice was forming in my stomach. I wished I could just put my foot down and say I absolutely would not work on this topic, but we were already committed. Besides, it would be difficult to refuse without giving a reason, and what would that reason even be? Lying about shopping for bras is one thing, but I couldn't think of a lie that could possibly work in this case, and I didn't really want to. Maybe I was just being foolish. Maybe it was all a crazy coincidence that Ms. Smithburg had suggested a topic that hit so close to home for me. Maybe it would be therapeutic to relive my strictly classified past. Maybe it would even have tons of *pizzazz*.

"Okay, fine, let's do it. I like the video diary idea, but

can we just do it with old photos and narration? I think that would work better for me."

"Why, are you afraid you won't show up on camera?" Eli laughed.

"No! I'm not afraid of that. Why would you say something like that?" I shot back. *Why would he say something like that?* I wondered. Does he think he knows something about me that he absolutely shouldn't think he knows? Of course vampires *can* be photographed, but most people don't know that. Does he know about me? Is that what he's getting at? My eyes darted from side to side as I worried that my secret was about to be exposed. Then I looked at his face and his sheepish expression told me there was no reason to panic.

"Well, you are very . . . pale," he said. "Your skin is fair. I thought maybe you were worried that you'd be too washed-out for video. It was dumb, a bad joke. I'm sorry." He wrinkled his forehead like he was slightly afraid I would punch him, but I was too relieved. He'd only been teasing.

"You *should* be sorry. If it weren't for your squillion freckles, I don't know if I'd even be able to see you right now!" I teased. Eli smiled and flexed his bicep, the better to display his spotted white skin.

"Oh, you like those, huh? You should see them in

summertime. They merge into one giant freckle and it looks like I have an awesome tan!"

I rolled my eyes at him, but then gave in to a giggle I'd been trying to suppress, before remembering that I am *not* a giggler. I cleared my throat and Eli became serious for a moment too.

"For real, though? I think this project would be okay if we did it with photos, but I sincerely and truly believe that if you let me put you on video, we could take it to a whole other level. You could tell the entire story with just your eyes." Right when he said that, his own watery blue eyes locked on mine for a second. Nobody in all the decades of my life had ever said anything like that to me, and I responded the only way I could, by looking down at my sneaker, which had a piece of rubber peeling off the toe that needed to be addressed right away.

Eli left soon after that, saying, "Promise you'll think about it, okay? I gotta go. Thank your mom for me."

I believe I said, "Yup."

Well, I did what he asked. I thought about it over and over again until I was finally able to fall asleep. Now I'd thought about it all morning and the whole time I was walking to school and I still thought it was a bad idea. I also thought that if he made a corny joke or smiled at me or complimented my eyes just one more time, I would probably agree to whatever he wanted to do for this stupid project. I would never have admitted it to anyone, but the guy kinda grew on you. Ugh.

"Good morning, Jane." I'd been gazing at the sidewalk for I don't know how long, but now my head whipped up from the cement like I'd been caught doing something weird.

"You look very . . . pink . . . today." Timothy Hunt, one hand in the pocket of his expensive cashmere coat, held the school door open for me with his other hand. Inside, I was swooning over his chivalrous gesture, but outside, I'm sure it just made me look even more gawky by comparison.

"Do I? I guess I must. It—it makes sense," I stammered. What made sense? Certainly not me.

Timothy smiled. He was probably very accustomed to females tripping over themselves in front of him. As we entered the hall and walked toward our lockers, I concentrated very hard on not tripping literally.

"Pink suits you," he said. Timothy paused briefly but not long enough for me to think of a clever reply like "Thank you" before he said, "Listen, Jane, I've been looking over that article you gave me, and I find it very intriguing. I'd really like to discuss it further."

"Oh, sure," I said, and then dumbly added, "With me?" I realized I sounded like an idiot, and Timothy's bemused expression might have infuriated me if I hadn't absolutely deserved it. He put his hand lightly on the small of my back as we started up the stairs. It was just for a second, but the residual thrum of energy where his fingers had been lingered. I struggled to find some composure. "What about at lunch?"

"Yes, I was actually hoping we could talk somewhere a bit more private than the cafeteria." Before I could even start to tell myself that my earlier fears were true and that he was, in fact, ashamed to be seen with me, he added: "I'm not sure if you realize this, but Astrid is horrible."

Caught off guard, I laughed through my nose inelegantly.

"I'm pretty sure if she sees us in the cafeteria together," Timothy said, "she'll do whatever she can to be obnoxious and disruptive. What about second period?"

"Um, I have English. AP. AP English." Like I needed to be that specific, making sure he knew that I wasn't going to be in just any English class, but Advanced Placement English class. I'm sure the more I spoke, the more he was dazzled by exactly how advanced my English skills were. Or not.

"I have government. Why don't we skip our classes and meet on the football field under the bleachers?"

"Oh. I've never cut class before. Except for yesterday, kind of. But I haven't even found out if I'm in trouble for that yet. What will happen if I do it again?"

"Well," Timothy said, "the worst-case scenario is that you'll fall into a pattern of delinquency and have to repeat the tenth grade. Can you imagine anything worse than repeating the tenth grade? Egads!" He chuckled at his inside joke as he deposited me in front of my locker and continued walking toward his own. I watched him move lithely through the sea of students milling in the hall, and because I couldn't take my eyes off him, I clearly saw when he turned and silently mouthed to me, "See you then."

# seven

**As I walked into my first-period American history class, my mind was still racing with the idea that I could actually just cut a class and meet up with Timothy if I wanted to.** Grateful that our chairs were arranged neatly in rows rather than in any kind of group, I snagged the last remaining seat on the non-windowed side of the classroom in the fourth row as the warning bell rang. In my peripheral vision, I noticed some motion from the sunny side of the room. Between my perpetually fingerprinty glasses and having to squint because of the intense morning light, I couldn't exactly see who the frantically gesturing figure was, but logic told me that it had to be Eli Matthews, beckoning me to sit closer to him. What a goon. Still, it was kind of nice that he had saved a seat for me. I couldn't remember the last time anyone had saved a seat for me, or if anyone ever had at all. Either way, I couldn't risk sitting by the window for an entire hour, not with that sun streaming in. I pretended to sort through my binder on the desktop.

Everyone was sitting in their seats fairly quietly when the final bell rang. Though Ms. Smithburg was not at her desk in the front of the classroom, it was reasonable to expect that she would come through the door momentarily. However, as the clock ticked off five minutes, the students gradually became more and more restless, eventually speaking to each other at full volume, wondering if Ms. Smithburg was out for the day, and if we would have a substitute or if we should just go to the cafeteria. Though I didn't join the conversation, I was wondering what was going on as much as anyone. When Ms. Smithburg finally did sweep in at 8:06 a.m., you could almost sense everyone's disappointment at not getting out of class. I could also feel my anxiety level tick up just a notch.

Ms. Smithburg sat down in her chair without removing her long wool overcoat or setting down her chic leather briefcase. As she addressed us, her eyes never moved from the surface of her desk. "Good morning, everyone. I realize that I am late. I was attending to a . . . personal . . . matter. However, I also appreciate that your time is precious and . . . I apologize for wasting it. Please, open your textbooks to chapter nine. You will read silently for the remainder of the period."

Many curious glances were exchanged. Silent reading was a very out-of-character assignment to get from Ms. Smithburg, a woman who treated the front of her classroom like the stage of a theater. Still, everyone got out their books and did what she'd instructed. I paused partway into the first paragraph, about the Battle at Chancellorsville, to glance up at Ms. Smithburg, who had stood to hang her coat and stow her bag and was now smoothing her shiny, coppery-red hair in front of her storage closet. Were her hands shaking? As she turned away from the cupboard, I dropped my eyes down to my book and tried to look absorbed. Truthfully, though, the Civil War was losing the battle for my attention this morning. My head was buzzing as I thought about what Ms. Smithburg's personal matter could possibly have been and why she was acting so strangely. When I got tired of asking myself those questions, I'd switch to thinking about meeting Timothy Hunt for a private conversation instead of going to English class, and then my head would start spinning. Thanks to my double shot of breakfast, it seemed that my brain was able to obsess and freak out even more effectively than normal.

Fifty-four minutes crawled by, and though I looked up at the clock at least once a minute, when the bell finally rang, it still managed to scare me half to life. Despite being nervous about sneaking out to meet Timothy, my strong desire to get out of Charlotte Smithburg's class had me snatching up my belongings and stuffing them into my bag. Just as I was about to make a dash for the door, I felt a tap on my back. I turned to see Eli Matthews, not smiling so much as grimacing anxiously. "Hey, Jane! I saved a seat for you, but I guess . . ."

I knew it had been him waving to me, and I felt guilty for ignoring him, but if I had sat next to him and in the path of a bright sunbeam, I would have been feeling a whole lot worse. Not to mention potentially looking like a bubbling cheese pizza. Still, I wanted to put him out of his misery. "Oh, you did? I didn't see you, I guess. I really need to get my eyes checked, but I'm paranoid that the doctor will tell me I need stronger glasses." That was at least partially true. I was paranoid of doctors, with their stethoscopes and blood pressure cuffs and scientific knowledge. I was pretty sure that even an optometrist's instruments would quickly reveal that I wasn't exactly normal. But my vision was just as good as it had been for the past seventy-five years . . . which is to say, not very good. I got by with off-the-rack drugstore reading glasses. Not very stylish, but no prescription required.

My half lie did the trick, and Eli's face brightened noticeably. "Oh. You shouldn't worry about getting new glasses. You could get some really cool ones. Not that the ones you have now aren't cool. They are. Cool." Unsure how to respond to that, I just started walking. Eli kept up. When we got to the doorway and realized we couldn't both fit through at once, we did an awkward little dance that resulted in Eli holding his arm out to signal me to pass. I thought it was sort of gentlemanly, but I also heard someone behind us snicker. Eli didn't seem to notice.

I tried to hurry to my locker, but it didn't feel like Eli was in a big rush to get to his next class. I twirled my combination lock, pulled up the latch, and swung the chipped gray metal door open as he talked.

"I'm just glad you weren't avoiding me or anything," he said. "I was worried you thought I smelled bad or something."

I deposited my books on the shelf and slung my backpack, now empty save for a few pens and scraps of paper, over one shoulder. Eli looked at me hopefully.

"What?" I asked distractedly.

"I was kidding. About smelling. But you didn't say anything and now I'm paranoid. That I might actually smell." The corner of his mouth tugged down in an uneasy half frown and his nose twitched. He may have been subconsciously trying to sniff himself. I lifted my hand, then stopped myself, then made myself put my hand on his shoulder. I couldn't believe I was purposely touching this boy. The fabric of his cotton shirt felt warm and soft, despite being dotted with little linty knobs. He looked at my hand, then back up at me, and I could tell he was flexing his arm for my benefit. I sucked in my lips so I wouldn't smile.

"You don't smell," I said. "Well . . . you do have a smell, but that smell is okay. A little like cookies and cologne." What was I saying? All of my efforts to appear normal and I was about to undo everything by telling some kid he smelled like cookies? Suddenly, I became overwhelmingly self-conscious and I snatched my hand away from his shoulder and started walking quickly toward the school's side staircase that would lead me to the exit doors nearest the stadium.

Behind me, I heard Eli clear his throat. Then he was jogging up next to me. "Boy, Smithburg really seemed out of it today, huh? I wonder what's going on with . . ." Eli stopped walking and talking and looked at me quizzically. "Wait. Where are we going?"

I paused and looked at him. "Where are *you* going?"

"I was walking you to English because I wanted to talk about last night. . . . I mean, I wanted to know if you had time to think about it. Our Dust Bowl video. But you're going the wrong way," Eli said, jerking his thumb in the opposite direction as if gently pointing out to me that I'd lost my mind.

"Oh. I'm not going to English. I'm—" I looked around to make sure nobody was listening to us. As if anyone *would* listen to us. "I'm actually cutting class. Because I've gotta—I've gotta meet someone. He'll be waiting for me."

Something flickered across Eli's face that I didn't quite recognize. Was it disappointment in my delinquent ways? Annoyance that I wasn't taking our project seriously? Could it have been a bit of envy for whomever I was stealing away to meet? I hadn't really ever been in close proximity to jealousy before, so I wasn't sure I'd recognize it if it bit me on the neck. However, the idea that it could be true? It kind of thrilled me in a sick and selfish way I hadn't yet experienced. I liked it.

"Okay, well, then . . . I'll see you." Eli started to turn in the direction of the English class he wouldn't be walking me to, but I reached out impulsively and grabbed his elbow. Realizing that I might be hovering dangerously close to glamouring territory, I tried to hold back my emotions because I wanted our conversation to be real. It felt like holding my breath.

"I've thought about it, though, and I'll do it," I blurted.

"Do what?" he asked a little sharply. Well, his snappishness confirmed that I wasn't trancing him, but whether it was through my efforts at control or because I was weak sauce, I did not know.

"The video project," I said. "I've thought about it, and I've decided I'll do it." I grinned at him and expected him to smile back, grateful for my news, but he still looked kind of pissed. I hated that look.

"Oh, great. I'm glad you decided that," Eli said. I detected a note of sarcasm in his voice. Actually, it wasn't just one note. It was more like an entire symphony. Ouch. "I better get to class." He pulled his arm away from my hand.

"Okay," I said. "Can we get together later and start writing our script? At lunch?" I was trying to sound enthusiastic, a tone I was unaccustomed to. I worried it was coming out manic and shrill.

"Whatever you say," said Eli. "You. Are. The boss." He turned and strode away as the warning bell for second period rang.

"Thanks for walking me," I called after him. He swung his head back and nodded curtly as he continued on his way. I watched him for a moment as the hallway emptied and students filed into their classrooms. When the final bell rang, I was standing in the middle of the corridor, alone. It was nearly silent. Under different circumstances, I'm sure my heart would have been pounding. I paused at the top of the stairs before hurtling down to the bottom, where I pushed the steel bar that unlatched the door that led outside. I half expected some alarm to go off and alert the authorities that someone was trying to escape, but then I remembered I'd walked out just the day before, and as of yet, nobody seemed to have noticed. I stepped outside and broke into what I hoped was a casual but purposeful trot across the grounds. I tried to put some distance between myself and the weird feeling I had from the conversation with Eli in the hall.

When I got to the football field it was empty. That was a load off my mind. I had been worried that I'd arrive to find a gym-class game of touch football or a marching-band practice going on, but all I saw was the sun glinting off the field goals, forcing me to shield my eyes with my hand, and a tall bank of bleachers without so much as a soul jogging up or down the stairs. I slowed to a walk so I could catch my breath and not be sucking wind when I came face to face with Timothy. Pitiful. I never thought much about exercising because it wouldn't do anything to change my painfully sticklike appearance, but now I wondered if jogging might help me build endurance. I'd have to ask Zach about that one. Maybe he'd even have an interesting answer after he finished laughing his head off.

I walked around to the backside of the big cement bleachers. The shade made it instantly more comfortable to stop squinting like a mole and I opened my eyes wide.

There, on a built-in bench by the center entrance stairs, Timothy spotted me and waved. Even though the wind was blocked by the walls, I quivered. Weird. I'd read that quivering sometimes could happen at a time like this, but I'd never actually had it happen to me. I waved back, then not knowing what else to do with my hands, stuffed them into the front pockets of my jeans and walked over. Timothy, I thought, looked genuinely glad to see me. Quiver. Quiver. Quiver.

"Jane, you did it!" he said. "Are you sure nobody followed you?"

I whirled around frantically to check behind me before I realized that he was kidding. So dumb! I turned back slowly, and Timothy laughed. His laugh sounded kind of like he was saying, "Ho, ho, ho." It was low and sure, not nervous and tittery like my laugh would have been at the moment, had I been able to laugh at myself.

"I'm sorry," he said, making a slightly pouty face at me, like people sometimes do to a little child who's fallen down. Coming from someone else, I might have taken it as condescending, but when Timothy did it, I found it endearing. Even though we looked around the same age, the truth is that I was probably very young compared to Timothy. I realized that I didn't even have a vague idea of what his real "age" was.

"Please. Sit," he said, gesturing to the bench. I took off my backpack, dropping it on the ground, before sitting a full two feet down the bench from Timothy as he reached underneath his soft cashmere coat and into his shirt pocket to retrieve the tattered printout we'd met to discuss. When he noticed where I'd perched, he said, "Jane, come closer. I don't bite." Of course, telling someone "I don't bite" is something people say to each other all the time when they're trying to be funny, but it never really is funny. It's just a dumb figure of speech—unless a vampire offhandedly says it to another anxious vampire. Then it's hilarious. I cracked up, which seemed to delight Timothy, who laughed as well. I instantly decided that I preferred it when he laughed with me, rather than at me. I also instantly decided that he and I laughing together was something I liked very, very much.

"Thank you for sharing this information with me," he said, noting the article in his thin, white hand. "Do you believe that what it says could actually be possible?"

I took the article from him and looked down at it. Did I believe it was possible? Years of being pragmatic had taught me to approach all things with a certain degree of skepticism. On the other hand, if you'd have asked me in 1936 if I thought it was possible that vampires existed, I would have called you "dingy." That's how we talked back then. It meant "crazy." Now the one thing I was sure of is that you could never be sure of much.

"I want to believe it's possible," I said.

"Then . . . you'd do it? If it were possible? You'd give up everything you have here?" he asked.

"Everything I have? I don't know if you've noticed, but I'm not really super-wealthy or anything like most of the kids in the vampire community. My dad works in a factory," I explained, wavering between shame and defiant pride.

"I don't mean money, Jane. I mean your family. If you could, would you leave them behind to go off and live a whole new life?" he asked. His intensity caught me off guard. "I'm asking, because when I became a vampire, I had to go off and live a whole new life. I've lived hundreds of years on my own, and not a day goes by when I don't think of the family I left behind."

I had never realized how lucky I was before. I'd never really thought what it would have been like had I become a vampire alone and my family remained mortal.

"But . . ." He paused, weighing his words. "But it's been a long time since I could actually remember any of them either. My family. I try, but it's just . . . There's just nothing there anymore."

Suddenly, I understood what he meant. If it were

possible to go back to being mortal, but my parents and my brother did not, there would come a time when they would have to see me die. Maybe in an accident, or by disease. Perhaps I would live another eighty years and die of old age, but sure enough, I would pass away and they would live on. At first, they might remember every little thing about me, but eventually it would be hard to think of what I looked like without consulting a photograph. It would become difficult to remember what my voice sounded like. There would even come a time when the number of years in which they had no daughter far outweighed the ninety or so years I'd been theirs. I gulped hard as I wrapped my mind around the concept.

"It's a lot to consider," I admitted. "But if it is real, I'd have plenty of time to think about it anyway. The treatment's gotta be really expensive. I'd probably have to get an after-school job and save up. Just convincing my parents to let me fill out employment applications might take years . . . but I'll bet it's like . . . thousands of dollars—"

"It is indeed expensive," said Timothy, interrupting. "I don't know of any after-school job that would nearly cover it."

I stared at him blankly. "What do you mean?" I asked.

"I've contacted him, Jane. The man in the article. His name is Dr. Almos Erdos. He's a professor at a university in Hungary," Timothy explained. My mouth opened and closed, then opened again but was unable to form any words. Timothy pressed on, "Dr. Erdos says the cure he's developed is ready and he'll be able to produce two doses with the money I've agreed to pay him. He's coming, Jane. I guess I should have discussed it with you first, but I wanted to surprise you. You don't have to give me your answer right now. You still have some time to decide." My mind reeled. Was he asking what I thought he was asking? Could he be serious? I searched his to-live-for eyes for a clue.

"How much?" I asked. "How much time would I have to decide?"

Timothy took my hand in his and squeezed it excitedly. "He won't be here until Thursday."

# eight

**I sat outside Mrs. Rosebush's office, waiting to be called.**
My parents were already in there. I jiggled my leg nervously
until I noticed the school secretary staring at me over her
reading glasses as she pursed her frosted coral lips. I'm
pretty sure the look on her face was disapproval. I wondered
for a second if she was somehow aware that I'd skipped out
on a class earlier, but then I reasoned that most teachers
probably turned in their class attendance sheets at the end
of the day, or maybe even the end of the week, if they ever
did it at all. Maybe people cut class all the time because it
was easy. Or maybe the vice principal was cutting me some
slack because of my supposed *eating disorder*. Maybe this
secretary and her frown knew all about why I was there.
What a vile woman, scowling at a girl with food issues. I
mean, I didn't actually have food issues, but she didn't know
I was a vampire who had had a bad reaction to a tuna sandwich and was just here because of a crazy mix-up. Screw her.

I had bigger things to worry about anyway. My meeting with Timothy Hunt had left me shaken and confused. I had gone there thinking that Timothy and I were just going to compare teen vampire notes. I mean, he was very smart and to call him the cutest guy I've ever seen would be an understatement, so maybe I was harboring the tiniest fantasy that we might become BFFs or even decide to see a movie together, but I didn't actually expect those things to happen. Then, when he'd basically asked me to run away and become mortal with him, needless to say I thought I was being punked. Seriously, I expected Astrid and her friends to pop out from behind a garbage can with a video camera at any second. But they never did.

"The cure is very expensive," Timothy had said. "But I cleared my accounts and I've accepted an offer on my home from a buyer who's been dying to take it off my hands since it came into my possession." Timothy had called where he lived a home, but I knew it was a mansion. Fine: I knew it was a mansion because I had done a little cyber-sleuthing one night and was able to find his address. Then I was able to use that address to find an online aerial map. And that online aerial map happened to show a huge castle-like house sitting atop a rocky bluff, overlooking the ocean. That's how most vampires roll. Prior to our conversation, though, I'd had no idea he was living in that big old house alone, and that he had been alone for many, many, many, many years. Thinking about it made me sad. "After the cost for two doses of the cure," he'd said, "I would have enough left over to get us started somewhere new. We could even apply to college together perhaps." He looked at me in anticipation.

"This is really . . .," I started, then stopped. Really what, Jane? Unexpected? Unfathomable? Terrifying? Thrilling? It was all of those things, but then Timothy probably knew that. "Why me?" I asked.

"Because . . . because I've been treading this earth for a long time and I've met a lot of people—and a lot of vampires who used to be people—but I've never met anyone like you. You're brilliant and you're funny and you're interested in things. You're the most full-of-life undead person I know. Plus, with your allergy thing, it must be more awful for you than it is for any of us. I've been hungry and weak before, but I can't imagine what it must be like to feel that way almost every day. The day we met, and when you were stricken? I can't describe it, but I felt like I couldn't breathe either. I've always wanted to take care of someone, and from the second I first saw you, I realized that someone was you. So when you shared that article with me, it was something I knew I wanted to do for you. For us."

I looked down at my hands. They'd been laced together

in my lap to stop them from shaking, but then suddenly Timothy had taken one hand and entwined our fingers. His skin was papery smooth and exactly the same temperature as mine. I felt the warm buzz of energy that happens when one vampire touches another vampire, though this was my first non-familial experience with it.

"Thank you for saying those nice things about me, but you don't know me very well. We're just kids," I reminded him.

"In some ways we're kids. In many other ways, you're an old woman and I'm old enough to be your great-great-great-great-great-great-great-grandfather," Timothy said.

"Are you sure you didn't leave out a handful of 'great's in there?" I said. Timothy feigned shock.

"Don't disrespect your elders," he replied, shaking his finger at me jokingly.

I became serious again. "I'm not sure why you wouldn't just do it for yourself. I mean, it's . . . too generous. Insanely generous."

"It's not generous, it's selfish," he said, pulling closer to me on the bench. "I decided not to do it on my own because I'm tired of being on my own. I'm tired of living like a barbarian who must choose between obtaining sustenance illegally or unethically, but I'm also afraid of changing. So no matter what I am or what I become, I don't think there'll ever be a girl who could understand me the way you do." By the time he finished talking, his face was very close to mine and I could feel his chilly breath on my lips. If I were a regular girl, this would be the point where I would have fallen under Timothy's hypnotic spell and become powerless over what I was doing, powerless to stop whatever he was doing. But I was not just any regular girl. I was a vampire girl, not helplessly susceptible to Timothy's charms. So I knew that I was completely in control when I brought my hands up to his cheeks, guided his face toward mine, and started making out with him so hard, it put the bragging girls I sometimes overheard in the locker room to shame. For two vampires with ice-cold lips, it was incredibly hot. Hot, except for how my glasses kept getting knocked askew by Timothy's nose. If I ever did become human? I was totally getting laser eye surgery.

Before we'd gone our separate ways, I promised Timothy that I'd think about it, but so far the thing I was thinking about most was the kissing. As unbelievable as everything else was, I still couldn't believe that the kissing had happened! Me. Jane Jones, tenth-grade vampire, had been kissed. And, as far as I knew, it wasn't even part of a dare!

"Ms. Jones. Ms. Jones!"

I looked up from my daze to see the school secretary staring at me again. "The vice principal will see you now."

I stood up, glad to have that woman's eyes off me as she busied herself with tardy slips, and I turned the knob to Mrs. Rosebush's office. On the other side of the door sat Mrs. Rosebush with her brown-and-silver wavy hair swept up with a pencil poked through to create a bun. She had a practiced expression of warmth and acceptance on her face and gestured toward an empty chair between my parents, saying, "Welcome, Jane." I sat down, apprehensive about what was about to go down.

"Thank you all for coming here today. I would like to start by saying, Jane, we all think very highly of you, and this meeting in no way signifies that you are in any sort of trouble. Rather, I'm hoping to establish a dialogue with you and your parents so that your experience at Port Lincoln High School is a positive . . ." Blah, blah, blahbitty-blah-blah-blah. After less than a minute, I completely lost the ability, or the will, to listen to what she was saying. It all started to just sound like . . . sounds. Nonsense syllables that meant nothing. Not to be disrespectful; I'm sure Mrs. Rosebush was a very kind woman who cared deeply for her students. It was because the whole reason I was here was a phony, fake farce and I had a lot of real stuff on my mind!

"So, you can see my concern," she concluded.

My mother looked nervously from my father to Mrs. Rosebush to me before saying, "Thank you for making us aware of your concerns. We should let you know that Jane—I'm not sure if you have a copy of her record there—" My mother's mention of my "record" made me slightly uneasy, since it was only a folder with our current address and contact numbers and was otherwise mostly full of false information that we fabricated and sent along to every new school I attended. It made us feel kind of like criminals, the fake histories and identities. Some vampires did it to distance themselves from any strange occurrences or disappearances of their warm-blooded former acquaintances, I'm sure, but most of us did it simply to fit in with mortal society. As it was, I lived in fear of someday running into and being recognized by one of my elderly classmates from the forties or fifties. Aliases were necessary to maintain our anonymity, and though I had most of my faux details memorized, just in case, there was always the danger of slipping up and raising some kind of red flag.

I gave Ma the evil eye, but she continued. "It should say in Jane's record that she does have a number of food . . . sensitivities. Allergies, you might call them, which we think explains what you saw . . . happen . . . in the bathroom yesterday."

Mrs. Rosebush picked up the glasses hanging from a gold chain around her neck and slipped them on. She flipped through a pile of folders on her desk, murmuring,

"Yes, I think I did see something about allergies in Jane's file . . . I just had it this morning. Where is that folder?" She looked up at us and shrugged. "Well, this is strange. It seems like Jane's records have just gotten up and walked away." She took one last look through everything, then waved her hand as if she could make the mess on her desk magically disappear. "Oh, it's fine. I'm sure we shall find it sooner rather than later. Now, other than the minor medical issue, how would you say things are going this term?"

Jeez, this lady really liked to get up in your business! Even though I'd never shown any evidence of having telepathic powers, which the rare vampire does have, I tried to shoot my mother a quick mental memo to shut it down now. No such luck.

"Being new in school is difficult, but so far, we're pleased with how things are going for Jane. She likes her classes and she likes her teachers. She's doing well and she's even made some friends. A few. A few friends."

Thanks, Ma.

"That is good to hear. On that note, I invited one of Jane's teachers to join us to give her perspective on how things are going with Jane. She should have been here by now," Mrs. Rosebush said, consulting the clock. "Well, maybe she's forgotten. Jane," she said, scribbling on her familiar little pink pad, "please take this hall pass and go remind Ms. Smithburg that your parents are here. She has a free period now, but she should be in her classroom." I took the pass from Mrs. Rosebush's hand and stood numbly. The last thing I wanted to do right now was walk into a room and come face to face with Charlotte Smithburg. Never mind having her sit across from my parents while they all talked about me. There are limits to the creepiness that even a vampire can take. As I stepped out of the room, desperately wishing I could turn into a bat and fly away, I heard Mrs. Rosebush say to my parents, "Strangest thing. I bumped into Ms. Smithburg this morning. She was running late, but I made it a point to tell her that you would be here and that I'd like her to come say hello. . . ."

The school's administrative offices were on the ground level, and Ms. Smithburg's room was just up one switchback flight of stairs. The walk certainly wasn't long enough to think of a plan for getting out of this, and I had already pushed my luck once today. I took the stairs as slowly as I could, then walked stiffly down the hall. I thought about stopping at my locker to kill some time but decided to get it over with. I opened the door to room 217 and went in.

It was completely empty. Ms. Smithburg wasn't there.

I closed the door behind me and walked past my teacher's desk to the tiny room that served as an office between Ms. Smithburg's class and room 219. The lights were off and nobody sat at the small table topped only with an ancient-looking green rotary phone. I stepped back into the classroom and was about to return to the vice principal's office and suggest they have Ms. Smithburg paged or something, when I noticed a fluttering on her desk. A paper had blown onto the floor because one of the big windows had been left open. Just as I stepped forward to close it, a metallic sound rang up from below, causing the hairs on the back of my neck to bristle. Shielding my eyes against the bright sun and sticking close to the wall to remain unseen, I saw the figure of a woman I thought I recognized wearing big, dark glasses and a long, elegant coat step off the fire escape below the open window. She strode across the teachers' parking lot and ducked quickly into a sedan. I couldn't see exactly what model of car it was, but I could tell that it was gleaming and way nicer than most of the rides other faculty members drove to school in. I'm no detective, but I was about 1,000 percent sure I'd just seen my history teacher making an escape. But why?

Figuring that Mrs. Rosebush was enjoying the captive audience she had in my parents, I decided to do a little snooping around before I left. Not that I would find anything. I mean, I was just being paranoid, right? The fact that Charlotte Smithburg had gone from being my favorite teacher to a sort of menacing figure and that I'd witnessed her fleeing the school at the very moment she was supposed to be meeting with my parents was all some kind of crazy coincidence that seemed to be getting crazier by the day. I sat down in her chair and tried the file drawer.

Locked.

I looked in the shallow center drawer. Lots of pens and paper clips and trinkets and doodads, probably confiscated from class clowns. I instinctively avoided anything bright and silvery, just in case. Did I mention that earlier? That silver is one of those things you've probably heard about vampires that is actually true? Well, it's trueish but exaggerated. Just like I won't instantly burst into flames if I step into the sun, my skin won't start to smoke if I touch silver. Not right away. Still, I've learned to avoid it just like you've learned to let a burrito cool before biting into it.

There wasn't much of interest in the drawer, but I did pick up a small yellow envelope that contained a small dull key. The kind of key that might open a drawer in that very desk. "See," I told myself, sliding the key out of the envelope and into the lock on Ms. Smithburg's file drawer, "if she really had anything to hide, she wouldn't have just left this key." I wasn't surprised when the tumbler turned and unlatched the drawer. However, I was quite surprised when I slid the drawer open and saw the sole item it contained.

There, sitting right in front of me, was a manila folder marked with stickers I recognized from the school's arcane filing system. On the tab was a computer label that said, "Jones, Jane."

I drew in a long, shaky breath as I picked up the very folder the vice principal had been searching for just minutes ago. I opened the cover and saw that the front page, a form headed with *Personal Information*, was torn, with most of the personal information ripped away. Now seemed like a perfect time to start talking to myself, so I went ahead and said, "What the—"

"Hello, Jane." I snapped the folder closed and looked up. Framed in the doorway was Astrid. She stepped in and walked toward the desk, and I noticed her eyes slip down to the folder in my hands. "What are you doing here?"

"I was just . . . dropping off a makeup assignment. I missed some homework." I fumbled nervously.

"Missed homework? How unlike you," she cooed. Something didn't seem right. Astrid wasn't in my American history class and now that I thought about it, I couldn't recall her being one of Ms. Smithburg's students at all.

"What are *you* doing here?" I asked, trying to turn the tables and regain the bravado I'd been feeling when I decided to go through the desk.

"Ms. Smithburg sent me to pick up some papers she'd

left. So, if you're done there, I'd like to grab them. She's waiting for me to bring them to her in the teachers' lounge."

Well, I knew that was a lie, but did Astrid know I knew it was a lie? Since I'd said I was here to drop something off, I couldn't walk out with the folder. Besides, I had a feeling my file was what Astrid had come to collect, and she'd caught me looking through it. Even if my file being there *was* an innocent mix-up and Astrid was there on an innocent errand, I knew she wouldn't miss an opportunity to share what she'd seen with the proper authorities, aka Ms. Smithburg. Soon I'd be known as a school-skipping breaker-and-enterer. As calmly as I could, which was not very, I put the folder back in the drawer and softly slid it closed. I wanted to relock the drawer, but I wanted to get out of there more, so I decided to just do that. I stood and came out from behind the desk.

"We'll be seeing you around, Jane," said Astrid, tossing her heavy hair over her shoulder. I walked quickly past her, out the door and down the stairs, never stopping until I was back inside Mrs. Rosebush's office. Mrs. Rosebush and my parents all looked up at me, puzzled, probably wondering what had taken me so long and why I'd come back alone.

"She wasn't there," I said. "I looked everywhere."

# nine

**No matter how many times I would ever walk into that stupid cafeteria, I knew my stomach would never fail to do a sickening flip.** When you're not considered hot or popular or . . . normal . . . the classrooms and hallways at school can be difficult enough, but for some reason, when kids are let loose in the cafeteria, they behave like monsters. Don't think I don't know how ironic that is, coming from me. I cautiously navigated between a tableful of lacrosse jocks playing keep-away with one poor mathlete's soup thermos and a gaggle of student-council girls selling red-and-white PLHS buttons. Between the boys and the girls, I was more intimidated by the girls. They looked like if they didn't raise enough money *and* school spirit, they'd take all of us down somehow.

Truthfully, even though I hated the caf, I was looking forward to seeing Eli. After the roller-coaster day I'd had so far, I would be happy to just sit and work for a little while with someone who, I was realizing more and more, was always utterly dependable even if he was probably still mad at me. I scanned the tables looking for Eli's broad shoulders and the top of his gingery brush cut bent over some books. At first, I didn't see him, but when I looked around again, I spotted him in a far corner of the room, sitting down, looking up into the face of a girl, smiling and chatting. That flip my stomach had done just a minute ago was only a warm-up. Now it was going for a round-off–back handspring with a full dismount. Even at this distance it only took one flick of her gleaming chestnut waves for me to realize the girl he was talking to was Astrid.

We learned in biology about the fight-or-flight response that's triggered in animals when they are threatened. Right then, I wanted to get the first flight to anywhere else like you wouldn't believe. I certainly didn't feel up for a fight. Maybe in vampires, a third reaction exists in which you stare daggers at another vampire and see if they get the hint to go the hell away. I guess I was about to find out. I smoothed my own dull brown bangs down over my eyes as I walked reluctantly toward them.

"Hi, Eli. Thanks for meeting me," I said.

"It's lunch. I would have been here no matter what," Eli responded in a monotone voice, without ever taking his eyes off Astrid. I could tell right away that she'd been

trancing him a little because although she had a coat
draped casually over one arm, she was touching his shoulder with her free hand.

I pulled out a chair and sat down. I had to get him to
look at me, so I picked up his hand and held it in both of
mine. It was really big for a kid's hand. I wondered if he
was still growing or whether he'd just stay the same size
from now on. Feeling the coolness of my skin, Eli seemed
to finally become conscious of the fact that someone besides Astrid was talking to him. What *I* felt was my own
power to glamour a human flowing through Eli and slam-
ming into Astrid's energy. "Still, I'm glad I can count on
you," I said to him, smiling softly as his eyes adjusted to
my face. Astrid looked shocked, and pissed. I'm sure she
assumed that because I was blood-intolerant that I wasn't
like normal vampires in mostly every other way. Well,
when you assume, Astrid, you make an *a-s-s* out of *u, u, u*!
I'll give her credit, though—she was able to recover almost
instantly.

"Jane," she cooed, jerking her hand away from Eli
like he was a hot stovetop, "I was just here talking to
Eli because I was looking for you! I wanted to make sure
you were okay." She paused for dramatic effect. "I know
you had that big . . . meeting . . . in the vice principal's office today." She scrunched her perfect eyebrows in an ex-

pression of affected concern. "I think you are so *brave* to admit you have this disorder and that you want to get help. Are they going to send you to, like, a psychiatric hospital or something?" Eli looked from Astrid to me, obviously confused.

"How did you know about that meeting?" I snapped.

"Oh, Jane," she said, "there isn't much that happens inside the walls of this school that I don't know about. Or outside the walls, for that matter." She laughed before leveling her cold green gaze at me. "I work in the office during my study period. In fact, if you play your cards right, today's attendance sheet from your English class could wind up missing. You'd like that, right? Since you were too busy having a little rendezvous to make it to class?" She winked slyly at Eli, who reddened and lowered his eyes to his notebook.

"Thanks," I said, "but I wouldn't want to owe you anything."

Astrid shrugged and unrolled the coat she'd been carrying over her arm, throwing it over her shoulders. It was a man's navy cashmere blazer that I'd last seen when Timothy had slipped Dr. Erdos's article into the inner pocket. "Have it your way," she said, making a big show of turning up the collar around her face. She was enjoying this.

"Nice jacket," I said, not at all sincerely.

"Oh, this? It's Tim's. I was freezing, so I grabbed it out of his locker," she prattled. Then, to Eli, she said, "Timothy and I used to sort of be together, so we shared a locker. It was totally casual, but now it's over and we're just friends." Again, Eli reddened and averted his eyes. "Anyway, I was looking for a sweater or something and was surprised to see he left this coat in there. Kind of careless, if you ask me. I'm not sure you can exactly trust everyone at this school." As she spoke, she looked at me and patted her side where I knew the jacket's inner pocket was, the pocket that held the article I'd given to Timothy.

My breath became very shallow and panicky. If sweating had been something I did much, my palms would have been slick. Instead, I felt a painful shock in both of my hands as Astrid put her fingers up to Eli's cheek, caressing it. "See how cold I am? I can never get warm! That's why I was saying, before Jane got here, that maybe instead of a football game, you could take me to a movie. How's Friday?"

"Friday. Friday . . . is good. Okay," droned Eli. The second Astrid removed her hand, the current between the three of us stopped humming. Clearly, she'd wanted to show me that maybe I'd made an assumption about exactly how powerful she was. Point taken.

"Then I'll see you Friday," she purred, turning on the

heel of her premium-leather boot. She began to walk away before tossing one last remark over her shoulder at me. "And about your . . . disorder . . . Jane? I might know of this Hungarian doctor who's come up with a cure."

We both watched her walk away, before Eli turned to me, the fogginess slowly disappearing from his eyes. If he had still been upset with me, his annoyance seemed now to be outweighed by concern. For me. After a moment, he said, "What disorder? What was she talking about, Jane? Are you okay?"

I wasn't. I wasn't okay at all. Between our earlier run-in in Ms. Smithburg's room and her showing up here with Timothy's jacket, throwing around words like *doctor* and *cure*, Astrid had delivered her message loud and clear. Though she couldn't know everything, she knew at least something about Timothy's plan and my involvement and she was not going to just go away. "I . . . I . . . um," I faltered, trying to come up with something, anything, to say to Eli.

"You're crying," Eli whispered.

Astonished, my hand flew up to my face. For the first time in I couldn't remember how long, a lone fat, salty teardrop was rolling down my cheek. I wiped at it and looked at my fingers, relieved to see just a glistening, clear wetness. Obviously, my huge meal from the morning had been enough to help produce a one-tear meltdown. It was when Eli squeezed my other hand that I realized we were still attached. I also realized that, much like I had been sending these weird psychic vampire waves into Eli to help interrupt Astrid's vampiric whammy, he was now sending these weird psychic Eli waves into me, giving me the little bit of strength I needed to pull myself together. I looked up into his eyes. "I'm sorry. I have a lot of . . . personal . . . stuff going on right now. I don't think I'll be able to work on our project today," I said.

"I totally get it," Eli said, shaking his head. "I totally understand. You gotta do what you gotta do. Don't worry about the project right now. We've still got plenty of time."

Plenty of time. What a crazy concept. Up until now, my life had been nothing but roaming around and killing time. Now I had about forty-eight hours to figure out if I was brave enough to leave my family behind and start an entirely new life with someone I barely knew. Oh, and during the next two days of weighing my eternal fate, maybe I could use my spare time to figure out exactly why a teacher seemed to be dogging me, possibly with the help of her evil assistant, Astrid! Also, I had a French quiz that I was definitely not going to ace unless I studied. It was time to prioritize.

"Thanks," I said, slowly withdrawing my hand from

Eli's. He curled his freckled fingers closed on his empty palm like he was trying to trap the feeling of my hand inside his. I added another priority to my list: make sure Eli didn't wind up dazed and drained on a movie-theater floor come Friday night. Not if I could help it. I gathered my backpack and walked out the cafeteria door just as the warning bell rang to let everyone know that time was almost up.

Out in the hallway, I walked through the swelling crowd of students to my locker to unload my books and pick up my gym clothes. I looked at myself in the magnetic mirror stuck to the inside of my locker door. Even though I felt shaky and scared, my face looked cool and calm. I was formulating a plan that was so crazy, it just might get me close-to-killed. Or suspended! There was also a slight chance it might work, if I didn't screw anything up.

In the girls' locker room, I chose a bench near the back corner, where I quickly changed out of my jeans and into my sweatpants. I wasn't trying to be extra-inconspicuous just because I was on a mission, I was trying to be extra-inconspicuous because my bra was tiny and my underwear was eleven years old and I didn't want anyone to see me almost naked. I stuffed my jeans into my backpack and walked upstairs to take a seat on the bleachers.

My gym teacher was Mrs. J. I don't know what *J* stood for. I don't think anybody had ever dared to ask. Just as puzzling as the mysterious *J* part of her name was the *Mrs.* part. She wore no wedding ring on her thick, tan fingers and try as hard as I might, I could not imagine any person of any kind agreeing to live with her and watch TV with her and share a bathroom with her. I pictured her wearing her huge sneakers to bed after drinking raw eggs for dinner. She was tough and prickly, and I'm not even making a joke about her numerous chin hairs, which were not her fault but which also didn't help matters.

I had hoped to step up and speak with Mrs. J before class began, but I could see through her office window that she was leaning back, talking on the phone, with her blinding white size tens up on the desk. She didn't look like she was going to move anytime soon.

The bell rang and the bleachers filled with other girls as we all sat waiting for Mrs. J to emerge. When she did, an ear-splitting tweet from her silver whistle signaled us to stand. "All right, everybody. Get in five rows of five, five feet apart. We're going to stretch and warm up for indoor soccer." There were a few groans, but very quiet ones, as everybody walked out onto the court. I hung back and slowly sidled up to Mrs. J.

"Mrs. J," I said weakly, "I don't think I'll be able to play soccer today." Mrs. J looked at me through the brown lenses of her glasses, which were the kind that magically darkened depending on how bright the light you were in. They weren't dark enough that I couldn't see her glaring at me.

"What's wrong with you?" she asked.

"It's my stomach. I'm having really bad cramps," I lied. Actually, it wasn't an enormous lie. My stomach was churning, but it was mostly out of fear. Still, it was kind of like method acting.

"Oh, you've got your friend?" asked Mrs. J.

I looked around to see who she was talking about. "No, it's just me," I replied stupidly. One girl on the gym floor overheard and stopped her lazy stretching to elbow her neighbor. They both guffawed.

"No," Mrs. J said impatiently, "is your *aunt* visiting?" A little too late, I realized she was asking if I had my period. Of course, by now, every other girl in class was occupied with eavesdropping on our conversation while convulsing with silent laughter at my stupidity.

"No, I just have cramps," I said. I could feel the anger and humiliation rising in me.

"So you're *not* menstruating," Mrs. J finally said, so loudly that my classmates could no longer contain their hysteria. Their jeering made it feel like the walls were closing in on me. For a second I wished that I could turn on all of them and bare my fangs. I pictured myself sinking my teeth into this girl Ally McNally's spray-tanned neck while she screamed for her two best friends, Allie and Ali, to help her. And then what would I do? Go into a blood-induced anaphylactic shock as a bunch of humans snapped pictures of me with their cell-phone cameras to put on their Tumblrs? I needed to calm down and end this conversation ASAP so that I could get on with my plan. The old me, of a few days ago, might have backed down, but the new me wasn't such a wimp. If Mrs. J was actually trying to embarrass me, maybe it was best to fight fire with embarrassing fire.

"No," I responded defiantly, "my periods are extremely irregular. In fact, it's been a long time since I last had one." Mrs. J's lips tightened in discomfort as I spoke and the girls from my class had gone from shrieking with laughter to just tittering. Maybe they all decided I was less funny-crazy and more scary-crazy. Good. Because if you thought about it, I had something like nine hundred months' worth of PMS coming to me and now was as good a time as any to use some of it. I continued, even louder, for everyone's benefit. "The pain isn't in my uterus or pelvic area. My genitals are fine. But I *am* having some intense cramping." Mrs. J's jaw had gone slack from my graphic description.

"So, may I go to the nurse now?" I asked, with what sounded to me like an edge of actual menace in my voice. It felt awesome.

"Get a pass off my desk and go," said Mrs. J, obviously eager to shut me up. I tuned everything out except the squeaks of my Chuck Taylors crossing the polished wood floor. As I took a pass from Mrs. J's desk, the bleat of her whistle reverberated off the brick walls and steel beams of the gym. Normal PE activity had resumed, but I was out the door. The first step of my ten-step mission had been a less-than-rousing success, but I'd done it. Step two was figuring out what steps three through ten actually were.

# ten

**I heard a knock on my bedroom door and before I even had a chance to say,** "Yeah?" Zachary barged in, pushed open the dark drapes on my canopy bed, and sat on the edge of my mattress. I'd given up on hoping that his manners would improve decades ago. "Hey," he said, "I'm sorry I was a jerk at breakfast this morning." For a second, I was stunned, then I got wise.

"Did Ma make you come and say that?" I asked.

"Of course she did," he replied. "She was worried because you've been all mopey ever since you got home from school. She thinks it's because you're pissed at me."

"Not really. I know you can't help yourself," I said, mussing his already-mussed mop of hair.

"But I am sorry," he said, trying to duck my hand. "Hey, I've been working on another idea for your blood-intolerant thing, J."

"You have? Tell me about it," I said.

"Okay, so blood types are a classification of blood based on the presence or absence of inherited antigenic substances on the surface of red blood cells, right?" he rattled excitedly. "Some blood types make A antigens, some make B antigens, some make H antigens, which is important because in order to receive, like, a blood donation, a person has to get the type of blood that matches the antigens present on the surfaces of their other cells and tissues, y'know?"

Honestly, he had lost me a while ago. I was a good student, for sure, but science wasn't really my thing. Maybe it's because I had learned the hard way that what science does not know about certain things is a lot. For example, a Nobel Prize–winning geneticist might tell me that I don't exist. Which, I happen to know, is false. I also never really enjoyed dissecting things, possibly because I've often worried about being caught and dissected myself. So, no, I didn't know, but I was enjoying listening to his squeaky little voice spout facts.

"So, when we were . . . you know . . . transformed, I think something went haywire with you that basically killed whatever antigens were on the surfaces of your tissues. Not sure how that happened. Of course, if you were willing to submit to a biopsy . . ."

"No, I don't think I want you coming after me with a vegetable peeler," I said, punching his arm.

"Ugh, fine." He sighed. "Anyway, my theory is that if I could find a way to extract some HH antigen from the Bombay blood we have in the freezer, stabilize it and grow it, then recombine it with common blood plasma through plasmapheresis . . ." He continued breathlessly, "Do you know what that would mean?"

I frowned. "I don't. Tell me in English."

"It would mean that we could have an endless supply of blood . . . of food . . . for you. You could feed on more than just a drop every few days. If it worked, you could feed all you wanted. Maybe put a little juice in your ca-boose!" he exclaimed. I smacked his arm. Brothers should not be talking about their sisters' cabooses under any cir-cumstances. "Well, what do you think?"

"I think I am lucky, and I also think I have the best lit-tle brother in the world," I said. It was true. My brother was loud and often obnoxious, but he had this incredible gift, and he chose to use it trying to figure out a way to make my life better. Not a lot of vampire *or* human girls can say that.

"I don't want to get your hopes up too high," he ad-mitted. "I believe it'll work, but it's gonna take time. Not to mention using up some of the Bombay we have stored for you. But if I can make it happen, it could really change things," he said seriously. He was right. Not only would it be possible that I might gain strength, it would also make purchasing blood products on the black market so much simpler and less expensive for our parents.

"I love you, Zach," I said, swallowing hard on the lump in my throat. "Now, if you'll excuse me, I've got some homework to slog through. Not everyone in the family can be such a brainiac."

"Okay," he said, getting up. "I'll update you on my findings. Let me know if you change your mind about the biopsy," he said, wiggling his fingers in front of him like a mad scientist in a scary movie.

I threw a pillow after him as he ran out of my room and closed the door, leaving me alone on my bed. Even though I'd already swallowed one lump, I had a brand-new one in my throat. Here my little brother had been thinking of ways to help me, while I'd been thinking of ways I might leave him and the rest of my family behind forever. Actually, if I was being honest, I'd been thinking of ways to avoid thinking about that so far. I knew I had to give Timothy my answer, and soon, but first there were a few things I needed to sort out. Primarily, what was the damn deal with my history teacher?

For someone who had, prior to that week, never broken a school rule, I'd sure made up for it in two days. I'd become a one-woman crime wave! Okay, maybe just a one-girl minor-infraction machine. Still, I'd gotten pretty bold. After faking sick in gym, I'd passed right by the infirmary and went to the main office. A shiver went through me as I remembered the horrible secretary looking up at me over the tops of her reading glasses.

"Is Mrs. Rosebush here?" I'd asked. "I need to see her right away."

"Mrs. Rosebush is at a school-district meeting," she said with her pouchy cheeks quivering. "She won't be back today." Snap. I had planned on Rosebush being there. I wasn't exactly sure what I would do once I got to her, but I hadn't bargained on dealing with anyone else. Especially not this nasty lady. But I couldn't really leave without getting what I came for either.

"Okay," I pressed, "then . . . do you know if she ever found my file? She said it was missing during my meeting today and—"

"I'm afraid I wouldn't know the answer to that," she interrupted. "You'll have to check back in with Mrs. Rosebush tomorrow." She went back to shuffling the papers on her desk and I stepped closer. She looked up, jutting her round chin out, not understanding why her dismissal hadn't worked on me. I leaned down, then reached out and grabbed her fleshy wrist with my thin, cool fingers and looked into her dull gray eyes.

"I'm afraid I can't wait until tomorrow," I said. "That file contains all kinds of private information about me. It's not good that it's lost." It was only my second attempt at trying to glamour anyone, and since this time it was for semi-nefarious purposes, my nerves were acting up. I felt certain that at any moment, this could become an epic fail. I really needed to work on my self-esteem. "You understand, don't you?"

"I do," she said dreamily. "I do understand." That was a relief.

"Good," I said, not letting go. "Do you think maybe it was accidentally moved? Is there a file-storage room here?"

"There is." She nodded. "In the basement."

"Then I need you to go," I instructed, "and see if my file was mistakenly put down there. Do you remember my name?"

"I don't know," she said, softly shaking her head. Of course she didn't. She knew enough about me to feel like it was okay to treat me like I was a piece of chewed gum on the bottom of her orthopedic shoe, but she hadn't bothered to learn my name. Either way, it didn't matter.

"That's fine," I said. "Just go down to the basement and look for my file. Do not come back without it. Do you understand me?" I let go of her arm slowly and stepped back. I'd hit her with all that I had, and hopefully it would last for a while.

"Yes," she said, standing up and getting her cardigan off the back of her chair. She shuffled out of the office trying to button her sweater, but she had missed the bottom hole. She looked sort of insane, and I would have felt bad for her if I had liked her even one little bit. But I didn't, and I hoped she'd be down there for hours, looking for a file that wasn't even there. If anyone found her and brought her around, between the misbuttoned outfit and her explanation that she was looking for paperwork on a student whose name she couldn't remember, I was pretty sure they'd at least make her lie down for a while.

Once she was out of the office, I closed the heavy door after her and turned the lock. I looked out the wire-reinforced window to make sure nobody had seen me, and then pulled the shade down tight. The office seemed so hectic every morning, but by this time in the afternoon, it was pretty quiet, while the students listened to afternoon lectures, dozed off during filmstrips, or quietly gossiped on the basketball court about the weird girl's freak-out over her cramps. I pushed those thoughts from my mind as I sat down behind the secretary's desk and started going through her bottom drawer, which was jammed with yellowed papers in browning folders. Was this the second desk I was ransacking within twenty-four hours? I was becoming quite the badass! I spoke quietly to myself as I thumbed through the tabs, "School holiday calendar, medical forms, letterhead, budget, by-laws, education board meeting minutes . . ." Cripes, hadn't this woman ever heard of alphabetizing? I didn't see anything that looked helpful to me. I closed the drawer and briefly checked the next one up, which contained approximately one old leather handbag, twenty pads of blank hall passes, and seven million pens.

I abandoned the desk drawers and turned my attention to the desk's surface and the ancient-looking computer atop it. There was a document already open, a letter of some kind, which I closed without saving *any* of the changes. Kind of mean, but I totally enjoyed it. Once it went away, I was left with a horribly cluttered computer desktop littered with little cutesy cat icons rather than the folder icons that normal people used. I scanned the labels until I saw one that made me gasp. *Payroll.* I clicked on it and waited breathlessly as the computer groaned and strained, trying to retrieve the data.

*Bibbibbiddibbibbiddibibbiddiboop!* The sudden, unexpected trilling of the top-volume ringer on the secretary's phone caused me to drop the mouse and clutch my throat in startled horror. There was no caller ID, and

I didn't consider answering it for one second. I did realize, though, that if it was a faculty member or someone else working inside the school, a non-answer might prompt whoever was on the other end of the line to visit the office personally, especially if the matter they were calling about was urgent. I needed to wrap this thing up fast.

The little hourglass animation on the computer finally finished and the payroll folder opened. Inside it, there was a document called . . . *Payroll.* Very creative. I clicked on it and waited for what seemed like another interminable amount of time for it to open. When it did, I breathed a sigh of relief on seeing what seemed to be a decently organized and reasonably complete contact sheet of every teacher and employee working at the school this year. I scrolled down, down, down to the S's until I got to *Smithburg, Charlotte.* Had I been a more advanced spy, I probably would have popped in a flash drive to download the file onto, or even just printed out the list, but I was new at this, so I went the low-tech route. Looking for something to write on, I remembered all those hall pass pads in the drawer and grabbed one of those, plus one of the less chewed-looking pens. Writing quickly, I took down all the information there was. Ms. Smithburg's address, a phone number, and a long sequence I assumed was her Social

Security number. I didn't think I'd need it, but I was pretty new to this whole espionage thing.

Once I had the information, I shut down the computer and went to return the pad of passes before deciding that they might come in handy and slipping them into my bag. I walked to the door and unlocked it but left the shades down so people might not notice the secretary's absence right away. Then right before I opened the door, I noticed something out of the corner of my eye: the control panel for the school's announcement and bell system. The announcements were made with a microphone that looked like a CB handset and the bells were all on an automated system, but they could be overridden with the buttons on the panel. I was seized with an idea. Of course, in order for that idea to work, I would need the small chrome key that fit into the small chrome lock on the panel. Lucky for me, that small chrome key could be found sticking right out of its lock. I bet the secretary kept it there so it wouldn't get lost. Not that I was complaining, but everyone at this school really needed a seminar on personal and professional security. I turned the key and was about to press the button that was labeled CLASS BELL when I changed my mind and pressed the one labeled DISMISSAL BELL.

Instantly, the sound that all my classmates and teachers were psychologically conditioned to associate with the end of our day rang out more than two hours early. I waited a moment for chaos to ensue, then swiftly skipped out of the office and into the milling crowd of students as bewildered teachers asked each other whether everyone should be corralled or allowed to leave. Before things had a chance to settle down, I was out.

Now, after spending my afternoon deflecting questions from my mother about why I was home from school early again, and my evening sitting down at the dinner table with my family—which was something Ma insisted that we still do every night even if the rare feast before us only consisted of three small glasses and one sad spoon—I was finally alone. My father had gone to work, my brother was probably under his bedcovers pretending to sleep while he read textbooks, and my mother was watching that show where they try to track down criminals with the help of viewers' tips. I was a criminal now. I wasn't sure if anybody but me knew it, or if I was in any way wanted, but I was reasonably certain I'd broken at least a few actual laws. I hated to admit it, but becoming a juvenile delinquent was kind of giving me a rush. Funny, because the only thing being a vampire ever gave me was a rash. Okay, a rash and diarrhea and potentially coma-inducing shock. But you still get my point about juvenile delinquency being a little fun.

Sitting down at my own desk, I booted up my computer and took the hall pass I'd scribbled on out of my pocket. I carefully entered the street address I'd copied from the school's payroll folder, 124 Water Street, Fairhaven, then hit Enter. After a moment, a map of an urban area popped up. I zoomed in on the exact building in question. There had to be some mistake. The address Ms. Smithburg had claimed she lived at belonged to a church.

# eleven

**Nee-neet, nee-neet, nee-neet . . .** I'd set the alarm on my cell to go off a full two hours earlier than I usually woke up and slept with it on my pillow. When it did, I was startled awake, but not before I had managed to semiconsciously bat it away with my hand, sending the phone skidding on its black plastic shell across the carpeted floor of my room. I launched myself out of bed after it, knowing I had to silence the chirping before Ma's eagle ears heard it from down the hall and . . .

"Jane," she said, peering through my door that she'd already opened a crack without knocking, "what are you doing up so early?" I finally found the button to halt the alarm. They say "better late than never," but sometimes it's not.

"I have to, um . . ." I paused, trying to formulate my latest lie. You'd think I'd have gotten better at it from doing it so much. "I have to meet Eli? To work on our project. In the school library."

"At five o'clock in the morning?" She stepped into my room, clicked off my droning heat lamps, and wrinkled her forehead at me in the darkness of my room.

"I'm not meeting him until six," I said. "But I didn't want to be late. We've got a ton of work to do, okay?" I doubted this would be okay with her. I prayed she wouldn't call me on whether or not the school library was even open at six.

"But it's still pitch-black out," she worried. That was a good one! I spent so much time gooping myself up with sunblock and covering every exposed inch of my skin just so I wouldn't blister and burn in the daylight, and she was worried about me going out in the dark? What was she afraid of? That I'd get run over by a car and wind up extra dead? I couldn't win no matter what was happening in the sky.

"I'll be fine, Ma," I reassured her. I tried to stand up, but my joints were stiffer than I'd noticed when adrenaline had sent me flying out of bed moments before. I grabbed on to my dresser and hauled myself to my feet.

"Janie, you don't look well. Are you sure you don't want to just stay home and get some rest?" Wow. For my mother to suggest that I miss a day of school, I must have really been in rough shape. I knew she was right, though. The stress of the past few days had taken a toll on me and my body was starting to protest.

"I can't, Ma. I gotta do this," I said finally, picking up my glasses and sliding them on so my mother could see how fine I was. She might have stopped talking, but she never stopped staring at me with a look that was equal parts worry and suspicion as she nodded and backed out of my door, pulling it closed as she went. If my mother had any idea what I was actually planning to do with my day, she might have tried to wrestle my weak body to the floor and hold me there until I promised never to leave the house again.

I looked into my closet and briefly considered dressing all in black, but then thought: *Yeah, and why don't you also wear a bandit mask so you can look really inconspicuous, Jane?* I opted instead for my normal uniform: worn jeans, a gray hoodie, and grubby old canvas sneakers. I knew from experience that you couldn't get more invisible than that. I ran my fingers through my hair and snapped a band around my messy ponytail. I didn't even bother to check the mirror and see what I looked like, because I knew the answer was "the same as always, but a little worse." I tossed a bunch of information I'd researched and printed out the night before into my backpack and zipped it closed.

Taking the stairs slowly, I arrived in the kitchen to see my mother had a place set for me at the table with my

spoon and a double-drop of warm Bombay. I hadn't expected that.

"Ma, I already ate this week," I said. "We can't really afford to . . ."

"We can't really afford to have you unwell," she said.
"So eat."

I knew that once defrosted, the blood couldn't be re-
frozen, so it would be stupid not to feed. I also knew that
the supply of incredibly rare and expensive black-market
blood we kept in our freezer would not last for very long
with my brother secretly chipping away at it for his experiments and me eating two helpings a few times a week.
I picked up the spoon and waited for my hands to steady
before carefully guiding it into my mouth. The metallic
feeling of the spoon and the metallic taste of the blood
spread out over my tongue and slid down my throat. Almost instantly, I felt a warm wave wash over me. *If I could
eat that way every day*, I thought, *how different might my
life be?*

"Thank you, Ma," I said to my mother, pushing back
my chair. I stood up and she helped me on with my backpack, peppering me with questions about SPF 100 and cell
phones and syringes, all of which I had in there, just in
case. She kissed me on the forehead with her own parched
lips and I felt a little shock, which may have been static

electricity or may have been a little of Ma's strong vampire energy passing into me. I recoiled, then instantly regretted it. Even though my mother was a pain, I could tell she was trying.

I left my house while it was still cold and dark and walked down my block, turned the corner, and arrived at the bus stop, where I waited. Hopefully my mother trusted me enough not to follow me, hiding behind trees and in bushes. I hoped she trusted me, because I really didn't want her to see me boarding a bus that was traveling in the complete opposite direction from where I'd *told* her I was headed.

I swiped my pass and took a seat. At this hour, the bus was nearly empty except for me and the burly driver in his blue polyester Transit Authority shirt, plus one or two commuters on their way to or from jobs that may or may not have been more loathsome than my father's. I looked at them in their drab uniforms, clutching tall paper cups of coffee and wiping sleep from their eyes, and thought of how tired my dad must be all the time. Every day I made sure to allot plenty of time for feeling sorry for myself, stuck at age sixteen, going to high school after high school. But seeing these people made me realize how selfish I'd been. These mortals were exhausted because of their long hours and backbreaking work, but with any luck, they might be able to save a little bit and one day retire and rest. My father couldn't do that. Year after year he toiled away doing work that was difficult or dull, just to make sure we had a safe place to live and sleep and eat. Then, just when he might have earned a promotion or a raise, it was time for us to move on and change identities so no neighbor or acquaintance would ever question how odd it was that his children were, in fact, not growing like weeds. He could never let anyone notice that we weren't growing at all. While most other adults in the vampire community lived off of old fortunes that seemed to never run out, my father had become a vampire with nothing in his pocket and struggled to get us to where we were today. He'd probably wished a million times that he could just leave it all behind, but fortunately for my family, he never did.

"Miss," the driver said, looking at me in his wide overhead mirror and rousing me from my reverie. "This is Fairhaven. Last stop." I looked around and saw that I was the only one left on the bus. I grabbed my backpack.

"Thanks," I said to the driver as he pulled a lever to swing the divided doors open for me.

"Don't mention it," he said, winking.

*Don't worry*, I thought. *I wouldn't dream of mentioning this to anyone.* I pulled up my hood and started walking the four blocks east toward Water Street and the old Waterfront Church.

Where the bus had dropped me off had been nice. Not most-parts-of-Port-Lincoln-that-I-didn't-live-in nice, but decent. There were some storefronts that looked prosperous, as well as some big, old houses that you could tell had once been grand and beautiful but were now divided into apartments recognizable by the multiple mailboxes hanging from their front doors. The fences were mended, if not recently painted, and the lawns were neat, if not overly big. Then, for every block I moved east, my surroundings became increasingly sketchy, as signs of decay crept in. When I reached Water Street, I was shocked at the number of abandoned buildings and boarded-up homes. It seemed such a shame that a neighborhood just across the road from a beautiful Atlantic Ocean sound could have become that blighted. The street was so eerily deserted that it seemed like even the shady characters you'd usually encounter in an area such as this had said, "No, thank you. I'd like to lurk in a slightly more upscale area."

I stopped to get my bearings and looked for a house that still had address numbers on the door. For a moment, I thought I was only in the double digits and walked a few yards up, but soon realized that the first house I'd spotted had been missing the third number. The ramshackle

Victorian I stood before was clearly marked 272, so I started walking down, wondering how many blocks it would take before I reached the church.

All night I'd been thinking about what I'd find at this church, if I found the church at all. I had to admit that I was half expecting it to be a dead end, a fake address used by Ms. Smithburg and a likely waste of time that I could scarcely afford. Then, when I turned it over in my mind a bit more, I wondered if maybe I *would* discover something. I mean, maybe it was just a cover address Ms. Smithburg was using, but I'd learned from my late-night Googling that, despite hard times in the area, the church was still operating under the stewardship of a Father Kilcannon. Surely, if paychecks and school correspondence for a Charlotte Smithburg had started showing up at his church, this priest would have contacted the school to notify someone. There's no doubt the nasty secretary would have taken the call, decided something was fishy, and then asked Ms. Smithburg to explain herself while she tutted and judged the whole time. Maybe I'd talk to this priest and pump him for info! The more I convinced myself that I might possibly have to pump someone for *anything*, the more nervous I became. When I reached a hulking, old Italianate manse with rickety and sloping wooden decks and stairs extending from every side, my instincts told me it might be smart to cross the wide boulevard and continue walking along the edge of the water, where I'd be less likely to be seen by anyone. The day was shaping up to be overcast and gloomy, but I couldn't expect the streets to stay deserted forever.

From the vantage of the shoreline, my eyes scanned each building across the street as the sound of choppy little waves rose from the water. Normally, I was a big fan of lakes and rivers and oceans, but you know how you always hear about rats leaving a sinking ship? This seemed like the kind of place where rats might gather to get on board a leaky ship in the first place. I stepped carefully to avoid any broken glass or rusty metal, but the main thing I was afraid of were some jagged wooden posts that were sticking up here and there, left over from a pier that must have rotted away. Leave it to me to be the first vampire in history to trip on her shoelace and stake herself through the heart.

When I next looked up, less than a hundred feet away, I recognized the silhouette of the run-down church that I'd seen on my computer screen the night before. In person, it only looked half as nice. I thought about crossing back over to get a closer look, but something told me to stay where I was and be patient. That something was probably me imagining my mother's voice saying, "Stay where you are . . . and be patient!" Whatever it was, I obeyed. Finding a relatively debris-free patch of ground, partially obscured by a clump of yellow sea grass, I sat down. I checked the time on my phone. Seven a.m. on the dot.

I made an agreement with myself that I would sit and watch the wide front doors of the church for fifteen minutes and if nothing happened, I would just get up and walk over. But when those fifteen minutes were up, I decided to give it another quarter of an hour. At half past seven, I decided that I could wait for an additional fifteen minutes. I was quickly realizing that when it came to confronting a potential nemesis, I was a procrastinator. When 7:45 rolled around, I figured that another fifteen minutes wouldn't kill me. I was in the middle of making a corny joke to myself about how fifteen *billion* minutes wouldn't even kill me, when something caught my attention. I flattened myself low to the ground and watched as an expensive-looking brown sedan pulled down the driveway next to the church and turned onto the road. It looked an awful lot like the car I'd seen Ms. Smithburg drive away from the school in yesterday, and the person driving it looked an awful lot like Ms. Smithburg.

# twelve

**For a minute, I just stayed there, stunned and hiding in my clump of grass like a strange animal.** I was really going to have to check out a church? I knew, rationally, that I could enter a church without bursting into flames like you might expect. In fact, a house of worship is a really logical place for a vampire to visit. It's true that we cannot enter a home without first being invited, which I like to think of as just having impeccable manners. (Though it's kind of hard to brag about your manners when you live off of unethically obtained body fluids. But I digress.) A church shouldn't be off-limits to a vampire because it basically extends a blanket invitation where everyone is welcome. Still, the thought of marching right up to a house of worship and demanding to know what Ms. Smithburg had been doing there had me so keyed up that my fangs were out! Of course, my fangs were also chattering because I was scared witless. Which I understand was pathetic.

I waited for a couple of minutes, just to make sure that I didn't see that brown sedan doubling back for any reason. I figured that Ms. Smithburg was on her way to school, but she'd recently demonstrated an unpredictable streak I found very unnerving. When I was sure the coast was clear, I stood up, swinging my backpack onto my shoulders. I'd begun to cross the road toward the church, when a bent old man in a long black robe walked out of the weathered and peeling double doors and stood on the front steps. I froze in my tracks. Then the little old man, who I guessed had to be Father Kilcannon, pulled something from the billowing fabric at the side of his robe with a flourish, and I instinctively hit the ground to avoid certain, instant death from his stake-shooting crossbow or pistol full of silver bullets. When I uncovered my face and looked up to see what I'd narrowly avoided, a feeling of terror washed over me. There stood Father Kilcannon, brandishing a balding broom and sweeping the church's stone stairs with all the ferocity you'd expect to see from a man in his eighties. Which isn't very much. In fact, from where I stood, the dust seemed to be blowing right back to where he'd just swept, defeating the aged priest in this particular battle. I stood slowly and brushed myself off, glad to be alive but resolving to watch fewer *Buffy* reruns, since they were obviously making me paranoid. While I still wasn't exactly sure who or what Ms. Smithburg was, I now felt that I could safely cross "vampire hunter" off the list of possibilities for this old guy. I looked both ways, though there wasn't a car in sight, and crossed the street.

When he finally saw me approach, Father Kilcannon looked up from his work and peered—with some difficulty, it seemed—at me. Although he hadn't shot me with his broom, I was still rightfully wary. Was he a friend of Ms. Smithburg's? Was it possible Ms. Smithburg had told him to expect somebody snooping around? Who was he? "Good morning, child," he smiled. His voice, soft and scratchy, had that dreamy quality I'd recently become very familiar with, like Eli's voice when I'd found him with Astrid and the school secretary's voice when I'd finished with her. Something clicked in my mind like a tumbler on a lock when you can only remember part of the combination. My instincts, still smarting from the embarrassment of a few moments ago, told me it was okay to approach.

"Good morning, sir," I said, climbing the three long, squat stone steps that led to where he stood and extending my hand. "Are you Father Kilcannon?"

The old man let the broom rest in his left hand, while accepting my gesture with his right. I knew instantly from his warm, slightly damp touch that he was no threat. I also got the feeling that, besides being old, he was also sick and very tired. Like he was being used up. I felt terrible to be using him further for my own purposes, but I had no choice. I concentrated and pushed some energy from my palm into his. It must have gotten his attention, because his eyes, which I could see were obscured by cataracts, tried to focus on mine. I asked again, "Are you Father Kilcannon?"

"Yes, yes. I am, I am," he replied flatly. I could tell it was an old habit of his, to answer like that, in a way that might have sounded playful once. "What can I do for you?"

I continued holding his hand, which might have seemed creepy to someone who was fully aware, but Father Kilcannon just accepted it. I also grasped his forearm with my left hand and stared back into his eyes. "I've been researching your church for a project," I said. "Would you be so kind as to show me around?" On my request, the elderly priest dropped his broom with a *clack* on the top stair and turned wordlessly to the double doors, pushing them open. He shuffled inside, and I followed close behind.

The interior of the church was dilapidated and dreary, but I could tell it had once been grand. The cathedral ceiling soared higher than I would have guessed was possible from looking at the church's exterior. The pews, badly in need of restoration, were softly tinted by the little bit of the day's dim light that could struggle through the dirty prism of what had once been magnificent stained-glass windows. The altar floor was covered in worn and mildewed plum-colored carpet and behind the pulpit was a huge pipe organ that looked like it might crumble if you touched a single key. As we walked down the nave, still holding hands, I wondered how and why Ms. Smithburg would insinuate herself into a place like this. I squeezed Father Kilcannon's hand and tugged his arm gently, so that he would face me, and I asked, "Do you live here?"

"Yes, yes. I do, I do," he answered, leading me past the lectern toward a set of swinging doors, then through them, into the small, dark vestry. We passed through another door at the back, but suddenly, it felt as if I'd smacked into a wall. But there was no wall. When my eyes adjusted, I saw that we were on the threshold of a tiny apartment at the rear of the building.

"Father Kilcannon," I said, "is this where you live?"

The old priest nodded faintly.

Shoot. Unless he invited me in, I wouldn't be able to enter, but I wasn't sure what the vampire protocol was for this kind of thing. Was the fact that I was glamouring him a big no-no? Could I simply ask him to ask me, or would that nullify his invitation? I had to try, but I decided it was safest to go the manipulative route. "Oh," I said, "I couldn't impose on you to show me your home." Even hypnotized and vacant-eyed, the priest couldn't ignore the hint I'd dropped.

"No, child," he said. "Come in. Come in." And just like that, he led me straight through what had been an impenetrable barrier for me seconds before.

The flat looked well appointed enough, but something wasn't quite right. It didn't look properly habitable. The lumpy sofa was covered with a big white tarp, as if it was just coming out of or going into storage. There was a sense of disarray that I wouldn't expect to see in the home of a man who struck me as tidy and efficient. As Father Kilcannon took a step toward his living area, he stumbled off the edge of the platform by his front door and would have lost his balance if I hadn't been holding his arm. But he said nothing.

"Father," I whispered, "you seem tired. I'd like to look around, but maybe you should lie down. Wouldn't that be nice?" I felt confident that even though he seemed under the influence of something when I'd arrived, I now had him in my control enough to let him out of my sight for a little while. If I hadn't eaten two helpings of breakfast that morning, who knows? He probably could have kicked my ass. I let go of his hand and opened a door I thought might lead to his bedroom. Something sharp hit me right between the eyes and before I knew what was happening, I was on the floor defending my life. When I finally got the better of my attacker, I stood up and discovered, to my horror, that I'd been fighting with a pair of antique skis and a long moth-eaten wool robe that had fallen onto me from what I now saw was an overstuffed closet. Maybe the priest wasn't as tidy as I'd given him credit for. I stuffed the items back into their black recess, pushing my weight against the door until it latched closed again.

When I warily turned the handle on the next door, I was relieved to find a bedroom behind it. What didn't relieve me, though, was seeing that the small bed had been enclosed with heavy, wine-colored brocade light-blocking drapes, not unlike those on my own canopy bed at home, but kind of glitzy and tacky for an elderly priest. When I flipped the wall switch, rather than a normal overhead lamp that Father Kilcannon might need to write a sermon by, the room glowed crimson. Every single light had been replaced with an infrared bulb. The effect was dramatic and chilling and, in my opinion, a little over the top. You can get bulbs nowadays that throw off a lot of heat without coloring your room like the bowels of hell. Suddenly, everything hit me like a runaway SUV. Ms. Smithburg, my history teacher and newly appointed tormenter, was a vampire too, and this was her lair. I was sure of it. She was a vampire with terrible taste in home décor who'd wormed her way into this poor old priest's life. The only questions I had now were why and why me?

I turned, expecting Father Kilcannon to be right behind me, but he wasn't. I panicked. Whirling away from the bedroom door and scanning the tiny apartment, I couldn't see him. As I ran for the door back to the vestry, something in the corner of the apartment stopped me in my tracks. There, lying in a heap, was Father Kilcannon. I let out a small moan of dread and crossed the floor one agonizingly creaky step after another. Then, as I looked down at his crumpled, ancient body, I saw that he was breathing. In fact, he was snuggled up on a pile of tatty pillows with newspapers scattered all around and a threadbare blanket drawn up to his waist. When I hadn't been paying attention, he'd taken my advice about lying down to rest and he'd done it in the little rat's nest Ms. Smithburg must have set up for him when she'd glamoured him out of his own bed. I was repulsed but relieved that the old man was safe, at least for the moment. I stepped away from him into the center of the living area to catch my breath.

Feeling a bit dizzy from my revelation, I plopped down on the tarp-covered sofa, hard. I hadn't expected it to be comfortable, but when I felt a sickening stiffness, I leapt up in uncomfortable surprise. My mouth, normally dry to begin with, became impossibly arid as I stared down at the sheet covering the sofa. I attempted to swallow, unsuccessfully trying to calm myself as I reached down with a shaking hand to grasp the white dropcloth. I held my breath and yanked the sheet, sending puffs of dust swirling all around me, and what I saw caused me to scream like I was a mortal in a movie being chased by a fiend. Lying there, with his hands crossed over his chest, was the leathery and moldering corpse of a man who seemed to have been dead for quite some time.

Embarrassed at how I'd reacted, I covered my mouth with my hand. I glanced over at Father Kilcannon, who merely stirred and sighed in his sleep. Then, gathering my courage, I leaned in closer to the poor dead man to see if I could easily determine where that biatch Charlotte Smithburg had bitten and drained him. My eyes skimmed over his neck but saw no wounds. I leaned deeper and cocked my head to examine his wrists but couldn't readily see any punctures. I was overwhelmed. For all of my years of being what I was, and for all of the times that I had almost become a nearly deceased decaying heap, I had successfully avoided ever seeing an actual dead body. Now that I was just inches from one, I finally understood what it was about being a vampire that I hated so very much. I wasn't a monster, but certain vampires among us were, and they always would be. Unless something changed drastically, I would never get the chance to show anybody who I really was, because vampires would always be associated with greed and the kind of destruction I was looking at now.

More sad than afraid, I allowed my gaze to settle on the man's face so that I could remember him and maybe anonymously report his death to the authorities at some point. I don't know why, I guess because I'd seen it done in a movie or something, but I put my hand out to touch his cheek and the moment I did, I felt a small but sharp charge in my fingertips and the man's eyes snapped open, staring up at me. If I thought I'd been scared before, I was obviously mistaken, because now it was as if my feet were nailed to the floor and although my mouth had opened to scream, no sound came out. However, the man, who I'd thought was dead and wasn't, managed to open his mouth and make a sound. And a smell. It was kind of a raspy, rattling, "Ahhhhhhhhhhhhrrgghh," accompanied by the slow but sure emergence of yellowed and rotting fangs. Turns out I was wrong about him being dead *and* about him being a man! Usually I like to try to learn from my mistakes, but this time I didn't really feel like sticking around to find out what else I might have misjudged.

I bolted from the rectory and back through the church and didn't stop until I was blocks away. I had never seen a vampire in that condition before and hadn't even been aware that one could exist like that, but I was sure that if he had been in any shape to stop me he would have. Now that he'd seen me, whoever the hell he was, and now that I knew about Ms. Smithburg, the time for hoping it was all a big misunderstanding had come to an abrupt close. I got on the next bus back to Port Lincoln. It looked like I might be able to make it to school that day after all.

# thirteen

**Arriving at Port Lincoln High after my morning recon mission at my history teacher's secret church lair,** I let myself into the school through the same side door I'd crept out of, and then back into, when I'd met with Timothy the day before. It seemed like years ago that I'd been so afraid to miss one class; now here I was just hours later, a hard-boiled truant. I stepped into the hallway, struck by how silent the passage was. Although it was ninety minutes before the first lunch bell, there wasn't a soul in sight, which kind of weirded me out. Maybe the school had been evacuated due to a dangerous gas leak. I sniffed the air, picking up nothing but the stale scent of yesterday's sloppy joes mixed with a ridiculous amount of hair product. While it smelled lethally toxic, I knew it was harmless.

I was here because I needed to get some answers, and the only way that was going to happen was if I confronted Ms. Smithburg, aka Charlotte Smithburg, covert undead sneak, vampire to vampire. The questions of where exactly and when exactly and how exactly I would find her kept pounding in my ears as I mounted the stairs. I needed to get to my locker and unload some things from my heavy backpack while I gathered my thoughts.

"And where are you headed?" a deep voice intoned behind me. I turned on the bottom stair to see a male teacher whose stern face I recognized from the halls but didn't know by name.

"To my locker," I said, controlling the quaver in my voice.

"And why are you not at the pep assembly where you're supposed to be?" he asked, lowering his chin and raising his eyebrow at me. A pep assembly? That explained why this place was such a ghost town. As if on cue, I heard a dull roar coming from the gym. Probably cheering in response to a stirring speech delivered by one of the coaches of some sport or other, if I remembered correctly from the thousands of rallies I'd been forced to sit and roll my eyes through. I breathed a miniature, undetectable sigh of relief as the teacher approached me, giving me a look that was more menacing than was absolutely necessary, in my opinion.

"And?" This guy liked to say "And" a lot. I could tell he was relishing our encounter so far, and I was surprised when he stopped short of delivering a sinister chuckle and rubbing his hands together. Just a few days ago, this fella would have had me squirming, but today, I saw him for what he was: a sad figure who'd studied and gone to college and worked his way up through the school system so he could fulfill his dreams of nabbing wayward students in corridors. He obviously got some cheap thrill from it, and I pitied him. But not that much.

"Oh," I said, digging into my backpack and groping for just the right thing. "I have a pass." Inside my bag, I tore a pink hall pass from the pad that I'd liberated from the secretary's desk and held it out. It was blank, but I knew that wouldn't be a problem.

"Let me see it," said Mr. Intimidating Eyebrow, reaching for the paper in my hand. As he grabbed it, I made sure that my fingers brushed the back of his hairy hand. Ew. The little snap of electricity that passed between us caused him to look up at my face and then I cocked my eyebrow right back at him.

"I'm excused," I told Mr. IE, "for the rest of the day."

He stared at me with glamoured-glassy eyes and a slack mouth. "You *are* excused," he said, as if he'd just remembered something he should have known all along. I could have just left it at that, but there was something else I wanted to say. I tried to think of words so eloquent and poignant that they would echo through this man's subconscious long after I walked away from him and the memory of our exchange was forever lost.

"Don't be a jerk to kids," I said. It wasn't poetic, but it would do the job. Mr. Intimidating Eyebrow didn't look so intimidating anymore as he nodded and turned away from me. I smiled with satisfaction as he lumbered back from whence he came, never to bother another pep-assembly avoider again.

The second floor was as empty as the first, silent except for the faint chanting and fight-song singing I could hear drifting up through the vents from the gymnasium. I stepped softly and arrived at my locker, dialing the combination and lifting the latch as quietly as I could, opening the metal door slowly and without making a sound. I was all set to dump some junk, then impulsively rush into my next rash decision, when I saw two rectangles of folded notebook paper alone at the bottom of my otherwise neat locker. I'd seen plenty of notes passed and pocketed in my many years of high school, but I'd never, ever been the recipient of one. In fact, I'd recently noticed that texting had all but replaced the paper notes that kids used to exchange. Not that anyone ever texted me either, but still, I'd felt a little nostalgic pang of loss for what I thought was the passing of the passing of those old-fashioned notes. Now here it looked like I'd gotten two.

I picked up the little paper bundles and unfolded the first. It was written in a spidery, ornate hand that was almost too ostentatious to be believable. It read:

Dearest Jane,

I had expected that you would need some time to think about the offer I have tendered to you. I understand that such a decision cannot be made lightly; however, decide you must. I have reason to fear that Astrid may have somehow become aware of our plan. While she is dreadful, I don't believe she'd be so malicious as to try and thwart us. Still, I had hoped that we could keep our arrangement with Dr. Erdos a private matter between us. My concern is that, out of injured feelings, Astrid may inform the community. That may, in turn, make things more difficult for us. Or perhaps it may not. In either case, the time draws near. I await your reply.

Eternally yours,
Timothy

Well, obviously Timothy hadn't received many notes either, otherwise he probably just would have gone with, *Do you like me? Circle "Yes" or "No."* I refolded his letter and slipped it into the front pocket of my jeans.

I unfolded the second sheet, expecting more of Timothy's calligraphy saying something along the lines of, *Dearest Jane, I am still awaiting your answer. Please remit forthwith. Ceaselessy, Timothy.* Instead, the writing was kind of inky and blocky and smeary. It said simply:

> Hey J,
>
> I know you have a lot going on
> and I hope you're okay. I hope
> I see you soon. I have something
> to tell you.
>
> —E (Eli. Matthews. Your history
> project partner?)

I smiled at his signoff. I wondered for a moment what it was that he had to tell me, but his mention of our history project reminded me of our history teacher, and that what I really needed to do was focus on why I'd come here. I couldn't put it off any longer. I emptied most of my bag onto the bottom of my locker, leaving it untidy for the first time since I'd enrolled. I closed the door and twirled the lock. Maybe I'd straighten it later. Maybe I'd never get around to straightening it before . . . before I still didn't know *what*, just yet.

I approached my American history classroom and let myself in. While I expected most teachers to be with the student body in the gym, the Ms. Smithburg I was now getting to know didn't strike me as the type to have a tremendous amount of school spirit. Though the chairs were empty and the lights were off, it didn't mean that she wasn't there. I walked past the blackboard and pull-down map to turn the knob to the little anteroom that served as her office. There, leaning back in the chair, with her patent pumps up on the little worn desk, was the vampire lady of the hour.

"Well," she said, in mock surprise, "if it isn't Jane Jones! I marked you as absent today when you weren't in class." She placed her feet on the floor and leaned forward on her elbows, boring into me with eyes that I once found friendly but now considered hard and cold.

"I was doing some research," I said.

"Oh, research? How very straight-A-student of you," she said in the same mocking tone. "Was it for your history project?"

I gritted my teeth and glared at her. "I know what you are," I said. If Charlotte Smithburg had been surprised by my big announcement, you never would have known it. She merely sat back in her chair, folding her ivory hands over the crisp waistband of her wool skirt and sniffed.

"Do you?" she said. "Well, you were bound to find out sooner or later. Frankly, I'm surprised it took you as long as it did. Your intellect may be sharp, but your instincts as a vampire? Woefully inadequate. But, of course, that could be because you're so sickly. . . ." That was kind of a cheap shot, but I decided to take one of my own.

"My instincts are working just fine, thanks. They led me to Fairhaven and the old church and the priest you've been glamouring so you can live in his bedroom while he sleeps on the floor like a dog."

This time, I noticed a little flash of alarm register in her eyes.

"Why not just get a house like any normal, responsible vampire with a job?" I asked. "Is it because of that dusty, rotting, half vampire, half corpse you're hiding down there?"

This time, she had the involuntary gasp of someone who is at least slightly surprised. Then she narrowed her eyes at me.

"That rotting half vampire, half corpse is my *husband*,"

she hissed. Whoa, now *that* was something I hadn't seen coming. Well, whatever. I wasn't here to talk about relationships.

"I don't care who he is," I said. "What I want to know is why you went from being someone I thought was a decent teacher to someone who's kind of a stalking psycho."

My words seemed to really hit home with Ms. Smithburg. Her fists unclenched and her pinched glare relaxed. "Jane," she said, her voice softening. She stood and walked around to the front of the desk and leaned against it, making a steeple of her hands beneath her chin. "I have been looking for you for a very, very long time. The reason I'm here—the reason I took this job—was because I needed to find you."

I wasn't understanding this at all. I'd lived my life pretty anonymously up until now. At least I thought I had. Why would anyone be looking for me?

"Why?" I said. "There are plenty of others like us in this world, if you needed some vampire bonding. And unlike myself, most of them aren't even defective. So why'd you come after me? To screw with me about my past?" I felt myself getting emotional. Stupid trace amounts of teenage hormones.

"I am truly sorry that I had to put you through that," she said. "With all of the aliases you've used and all the places you've lived over the years, it was difficult to be a hundred percent sure that you were even the right girl. I'd been down so many dead ends." Was she making a pun? Because it didn't really seem like a great time for puns to me.

"Then I mentioned the Dust Bowl to you and the look on your face told me everything I needed to know. I couldn't believe it was really you." She reached out her hand to touch my face, but I backed away.

"Well, it's really me. Congratulations. So, what exactly is it that you want?" I said. I'd seen movies where one person searched for years for another person, but somehow I doubted she was about to give me the keys to a castle I'd just inherited in Transylvania.

"It's not what I want. It's what I need. Actually, what my husband needs. From your family," she said. Again she moved to touch my arm, and again I stepped back.

"My family? What are you even talking about? My family barely has anything. What could you possibly need from us? How did you even know about us and where we came from and . . . and—" Slowly, somewhere in my mind an idea began to form about just exactly *whom* I was speaking with, but I was nowhere near ready to accept it.

"Jane . . . ," she said, "I know this must be very difficult for you to hear, but my husband and I were there that day. The day that your family—well, you know, was made. . . ."

"Became vampires?" I fired back. "You were there?"

"Your father invited us in. And your mother looked so worried. If we had done nothing, they all would have died. We were doing them a favor," she explained, circling back behind the desk and sitting primly. Something about the way she was putting things didn't sound exactly right to me, and it nagged at the back of my mind as she continued. "Now we need a favor from your family in return. My husband is sick."

This was an understatement. The guy looked like he was at undeath's door. And as far as I was concerned, he could stay there. The rage I felt for what this woman and her putrefying husband had done to my family was sharper and icier than any feeling I'd ever had in all of my eternal life. I balled my fists to keep my hands from shaking as Ms. Smithburg continued telling me things I didn't want to know.

"Many years ago, in the 1970s, my dear husband mistakenly fed from a human with contaminated blood. Hepatitis, we believe. He became ill and weak, and we were told by elders in the community that the only chance for him to become well would be to feed from one that he'd created," she said.

"So you spent years looking for me so that I could let your husband suck *my* blood as a thank-you to you both for making my life a freaking hell? Well, that is really too bad because, guess what? Never. Gonna. Happen." I seethed.

Ms. Smithburg sighed impatiently, as if I were a thick kid failing to grasp a simple historical fact she was trying to teach me in class.

"Jane. Josephine, actually, isn't it?" she said. "I spent years looking for you so that you would lead me to your family. Understandably, if one of them recognized me, they'd be . . . upset. But you never saw me, because on that day you were so sick. I remember you bundled up and dirty on a straw mattress, apparently delirious with fever and hunger. To tell you the truth, we thought you were dead already, or else we might not have left you alone. But we *did*," she pronounced, "leave you alone."

My mind reeled as certain things became clear while other things spun out of focus. When I'd seen Ms. Smithburg bolting from the school on Tuesday it was because she was terrified that my parents would see her and identify her. But if what she was claiming was true and she and her husband never bit me, then . . .

"How did I become a vampire, then? If you never touched me," I asked, challenging her.

Ms. Smithburg lowered her chin and looked at me with a pitying expression.

"Oh, dear. Your parents never had *the talk* with you?" she asked. "Well, this is awkward." Her tone became derisive again. "Let's see . . . sometimes when a man vampire and a woman vampire love each other very much . . ."

Now she was toying with me and I'd had enough. I stepped forward and leaned over her desk, to show that I wasn't afraid of her, when really, I was kind of afraid of her. A lot.

"Just tell me," I growled with bogus bluster.

"Oh, fine." She pouted. "From what I can guess, when your family woke up and saw what had happened to them, they must have become hysterical. And then when you failed to die, like you should have, they must have become even more hysterical. Then, because they loved their little girl and couldn't dream of living eternally without her, they decided to go ahead and turn you too. Unfortunately, what they didn't know then was that when an immediate family member turns another, it has terrible results. It's similar to inbreeding. At least that's what I've heard from some elders within the community. You know, your family could learn a lot from the community, if they didn't seem to love being such eccentric little outsiders. At any rate, their terrible error is certainly why you have that awful blood-intolerance allergy that's made your life so pathetic. It was a rookie mistake."

I felt like I'd been punched in the stomach and I could barely breathe. I looked down at the floor and clutched the edge of the desk to steady myself.

"The good news," said Ms. Smithburg, "is that you are useless to me. So you're safe! If I had found you and your family sooner, before my husband's health had declined so much, we might have been able to make do with just a donation. Now I'm afraid it will require more of a complete sacrifice. So I do apologize for that." I raised my eyes from her desk and looked her full in her wicked face.

"You stay away from my family," I ordered.

She leered and clucked condescendingly. "Such a fierce warning, Jane. But even if you were smart enough and strong enough to protect your family, the day will come when you're not there," she said. "We can wait for that day."

With that, the minute hand on every clock in the school lurched forward in unison and the midday bell rang. Ms. Smithburg stood up, smoothed her skirt, and said, "Class dismissed!"

Before I could think to do or say anything, she was gone from the office and I was alone.

# fourteen

**I banged through our back door and threw my backpack down on the kitchen linoleum.** I shoved my hand into the drawer where my mother stored our few kitchen implements and felt around for anything sharp. Nothing. Fine. I grabbed a spoon, flung open the freezer door, snatched the plastic zipper bag containing my supply of rare Bombay blood and slammed it down on the counter. I opened the bag and jabbed sharply at the icy red mass until a baseball-size chunk flew off and skittered into the sink. I reached up into the cabinet and grabbed one of the glasses my mother usually served the rest of my family's blood meals in. My solid blood blob wouldn't quite fit. Fine! I reached up for an old, cracked teacup that had been left in the cupboard by the previous occupants of our house. I wiped furiously at the cup with the damp dish rag that was hanging over the faucet, then tossed the frozen lump in and set it in the microwave to twirl around on the defrost setting.

Usually, I would step away from the microwave just in case it was giving off radioactive waves or something that might be harmful to vampires, but this time I stood right in front of it and stared through the glass as the blood melted and became a puddle within its vessel. When the oven beeped, I popped open the door, wrapped my hand around the cup and brought it to my face, breathing in the warm metallic scent as I prepared to—

"Jane, what are you doing home?" My mother, arriving in the doorway and seeing me, stopped and clutched at the front of her blouse in anxious surprise. "What's going on here?" Never in my life had I been angrier with someone. I wheeled on her and before she could say another word, I bared my fangs and poured the gory contents of the cup into my mouth, swallowing all at once. In my entire time as a vampire, the thought of consuming so much blood at once hadn't ever crossed my mind. Instantly, heat spread throughout my chest and limbs. My face tingled. It was undeniably intoxicating, and for the first time, I could understand the sinful appeal of gorging on some unsuspecting victim.

"Jane, what have you done?" She rushed toward the counter, picking up the bag that contained what was left of my food supply and examining the significant dent I'd made in disbelief. Then she dropped the frozen blood and grabbed my face, looking into my eyes. "What have you done?"

"What have *I* done?" I cried. "What have *you* done? Huh? Maybe you should answer that." I allowed my anger to boil over, and because of the surplus of blood coursing through my veins, it felt like flexing a taut muscle. Violent energy flowed through my skin and into my mother's palms, causing her to tear her hands away from my cheeks. Good. I never, ever wanted her to touch me again.

"Jane. J-Josephine, I don't know what you mean," she whispered, with a stricken expression. "Tell me what it is."

I stared at her for an uncomfortably long time until she finally had to look away and busy her stinging hands by putting the spoon in the sink and picking up my discarded cup. I was incensed.

"*What it is?*" I shouted, veins popping out of my neck like cords. "What it *is* is that today I found out that we're not the only ones who go around from town to town using aliases and being freaks. For example, my history teacher, Ms. Smithburg? Today I found out that that isn't really her name after all. Her real name might sound kind of familiar, though. I believe it's Ruth Pike. Does that ring a bell?"

The cup fell from my mother's hands and shattered, sending bits of broken bloodstained china in every direction. Seconds after the crash, my father came through the kitchen door, wearing flannel pajamas and a look of alarmed concern.

"What's all the racket?" he demanded, running a hand through his wild bedhead.

"Oh, Jim," my mother said. Her eyes were moist, which was easy for her, because she was normal as far as vampires go. She could make a teaspoon's worth of tears when she really tried, unlike me on most days. On most days all I could do was wish that I was a slightly more ordinary version of a disgusting monster. And now I knew just who to blame for that.

"She told me everything," I said. "She told me that I was as good as dead and that instead of letting me go, you decided to make me what you'd become so that we could be together forever. But what you didn't know was that when a blood relative turns a blood relative, I'm what happens. An abomination who can barely live but can't really catch a break and die either." My mother covered her face with her hands as my father put a protective arm around her back, but I wasn't finished. "You've spent so many years smothering me and being overprotective, and the crazy irony is that what I really could have used some protection against was my own mother! And Ma, you know the part that disgusts me most? It's that you never had the guts to tell me the truth about what you did to me."

"Josephine," my father said grimly, "that's enough."

"Daddy," I whimpered, "how can you defend what she did to me? How can you—"

"Magpie," he interrupted, leaving my mother's side and coming toward me. My mother uncovered her face and caught his arm to stop him.

"Jim, no," she said. He stopped and put his hand on her hand and squeezed it, nodding once, slight and sad. Then he looked me in the eye.

"Magpie," he whispered. "Your mother didn't do this to you. It was me. I'm the one who was too afraid to let you go. I'm the one who did it. I'm so sorry. I didn't know." I felt like the floor tilted and dropped away from me, and all I could hear was a sound like rushing water in my ears. My father closed in to hug me, but I threw off his arms, shaking my head.

"Don't," I said. "Please don't touch me." Though I'd felt despair more times than I cared to remember, it paled in comparison to the way I felt at that moment. For the first time, my soul felt as dead and cold as my static, necrotic heart. Everything I thought I knew was suddenly meaningless. I wanted out of there, but I had one piece of information I'd leave them with. I stared at the far wall and spoke to neither of them in particular.

"Ruth Pike found me because she needed to get to

you," I said flatly. "Her husband is sick and he needs the blood of a vampire that *he* created in order to be restored to health. They expect one of you to give your life in exchange for the wonderful gift they bestowed on you."

Although I wasn't looking directly at them, I couldn't help noticing their sudden, extreme reaction. My parents whimpered and clutched at each other, but I stayed hard, not allowing myself to show any feeling. After learning that they'd not only destroyed my life but had also lied to me about it for three quarters of a century, why should I care that one of them might be in danger? Let them figure out how to handle it, because I was done.

My father grabbed my mother by the shoulders. "Where is Zachary?" he asked, shaking her. She let out a frantic wail and started breathing in shallow, racked sobs. At the mention of my brother's name, the blood in my stomach began to churn and suddenly my palms were wet with a thin sheen of nervous sweat. It felt unfamiliar and gross.

"He didn't come home yet. He isn't home from school," she screamed. My brother coming home from school late was a fairly typical occurrence. Sometimes he stopped at the library to pore through insanely dense scientific texts. Sometimes he wandered into the scrubby pines to study the flora and fauna. Sometimes he missed his bus and had to walk because he was being bullied by kids who thought he was just a little nerd but had no idea that he was an elderly genius who could end their lives if they pushed him too far. But right then I started to worry that maybe that wasn't the case today. I started to worry that something was really, really, really, really wrong.

"Is Zach one of the ones that . . ." I searched for the question I was trying to ask. "One of the ones that Turner Pike . . . could use?"

My mother, who'd been pressing her fingers tightly to her lips, lowered them as tears welled up and clung to her long lower lashes. "Zach is the only one that he could use," she said in a raspy voice.

Before anyone could say or do anything else, I barreled out the door and down the walk, running as fast as a stiff, sickly, young, old vampire hopped up on too much rare blood could go, pumping my skinny arms and legs like I remembered doing once out on the prairie years before, when I thought a bobcat was chasing me.

I got to the corner, and before I could let my intuition choose the direction I would take off in, I saw two figures approaching from up the road. One seemed to be rolling and the other seemed to bob and skip. One was tall and broad and goofy and the other was short and scrawny and Zach-ish. All the adrenaline in me rushed out of a hole in the sole of my ratty sneaker and I crumbled to my knees, panting and shuddering with relief. I heard the slapping of rubber soles on the tar and when I looked up again, a long moment later, my baby brother was in front of me, with Eli Matthews right behind.

"Jane," Zach yelled, "are you okay?" I put my hand out, and he took it and helped pull me to my feet. A happy zap jumped from my hand to his.

"I'm fine," I said. "I was just catching my breath. Thanks."

"Well, what the hell?" he complained. "You scared the devil out of me." I laughed at him. It was so funny to see a little kid cursing and claiming you scared the devil out of him. I messed his hair and squeezed him to me, then held him out at arm's length and shook him a bit.

"I'm the one who's had the devil scared out of me!" I said. "And Ma and Dad. What were you two doing?"

Before he could answer, my parents came screeching around the corner in our old family Volvo. When they saw the three of us, my father slammed on the brakes. Zach and Eli glanced at each other uneasily. Despite the appearance that my entire family was made of lunatics, Eli didn't turn and run in the opposite direction for some reason. The three of us piled into the backseat of the car and took the less-than-one-minute drive back to my house in silence. When we filed into the house, I could see that while my father had thrown on a wool peacoat, he was still wearing his flannel pajamas and his feet were bare. I didn't even have the wherewithal to be humiliated.

Back inside the house, my parents never got a chance to speak before I started on Zach with the third degree. "Where *were* you, Zachary? Do you have any idea what time it is? Did you ever hear of a phone?"

"Jane, you sound exactly like Ma. No offense, Ma," Zach said. "What is the big deal?"

Eli, sensing that the situation might be a bit more serious than Zachary comprehended, cleared his throat. "It was my fault, Jane," he explained. "I was walking home from school and I ran into Zachary . . . Zach. He was telling me a little bit about his experiments and that he needed to get some stuff . . . chemicals . . . for his chemistry set, so I offered to take him to the hobby shop? You know, the place downtown? I figured he could pick up what he needed and I could walk him home. Mr. and Mrs. Jones, I should have had him call, or I should have called. I apologize."

My mother's arms were wrapped around Zach's shoulders like she would never let him go again. She nodded silently.

"No. It's Eli, right?" my dad asked. "Thank you for getting our boy home safe."

Eli looked down, stepped on the toe of his sneaker with the toe of his other sneaker, and cleared his throat again. Then he looked up at me.

"I figured if I walked him home that I might see you. I needed to talk to you," he said, turning slightly red on his neck. "I put a note in your locker, but I guess . . ."

"I got it. I just didn't have the chance to get back to you yet," I said. Zach rolled his eyes and my father pretended to inspect his cuticles. My mother, ever polite even in an insane situation, managed a smile.

"If you two will excuse us," she said, "we have some things to take care of upstairs." With a gentle shove, she shepherded my father and brother out of the kitchen, leaving Eli and me alone.

"So," I said, "what did you need to talk to me about?" I really had no idea what to expect, but at that point, nothing would have surprised me. Maybe he wanted to confess to me that he was a leprechaun or a chronic bed wetter. Either of those would have been great news compared to the bombshells that I'd already had dropped on me today, but Eli couldn't have known that. The look on his face was anxious to the tenth power.

"Well. I hope you don't mind. It's just, I can see . . . I can see that you've got a lot going on. I mean, I haven't seen you in school in a while, but the last time I did, I could tell you had tons on your mind . . . and then when I didn't see you, I guessed it was because of, y'know, stuff," he blathered, but I knew exactly what he was trying to say. "Anyway, I figured that the last thing you needed to worry about was a project that I know you weren't that psyched to be doing with me in the first place. So." He took off his backpack and unzipped the main compartment, reaching in, then handed me a sheaf of crisp white paper. "So, I took the liberty of banging out this report. It's a story, really. I wrote, like, a story from the perspective of a girl our age who went West with her family in the early thirties. It has a lot of details I researched. I mean, if you hate it, we don't have to turn it in. . . ."

I tried to read the first page, but the words melted and floated away from me, and suddenly, for only the second time in nearly a century, a tear fell from my eyes and splashed on the page, and I could tell that more were coming. I didn't need to read the words to know that I couldn't hate it, because although the story was sure to contain many painful reminders of the girl I had once been, it also was a gift to the girl that I was now. It hadn't cost an entire family fortune, but it also didn't ask anything of me in return.

"Oh, come on," Eli said, noticing my tears, "I didn't mean to make you . . ." I was happy to be crying and I didn't want him to ruin the moment by feeling bad, so I grabbed his hand and squeezed it, then looked up at him and did that thing where you're laughing and crying at the same time and you look kind of mentally unstable.

I pulled him toward me and rose up on my toes to wrap my arms around his neck and hug him. It occurred to me that his willingness to hug me back might be because he was being glamoured by me, but it was hard to care because it felt so good. I told myself to concentrate on not thinking about kissing him, which by its very nature constituted thinking about kissing him, possibly twice as hard as I would have had I not tried to not think about it in the first place.

You know what I mean.

Anyhoo, the next thing I knew, he had pulled his face back from over my shoulder and mashed his mouth down on mine, hard—possibly twice as hard as he would have if I wasn't trancing him, which I still wasn't sure if I was.

"Ow," I said, pulling my face away a bit.

"I'm sorry," he said, "I don't know what I—"

"No, it's okay," I whispered. "It just hurt a little, but . . ." He put his mouth on mine again, softer, and a kiss bloomed between us that was warm and electric. Being the experienced kisser that I now was, it was a familiar feeling, yet completely different, and I wanted to explore every note and sensation. Then, my brain came back to a vaguely familiar feeling, accentuated by a vaguely familiar taste. A wave of panic crashed over me as I realized what was happening and straightened my arms to push Eli away. He looked as scared and confused as I must have, though he didn't understand why. Me, on the other hand, I totally understood. When my thinking about kissing had caused Eli to smash his mouth into mine, the sharp wires of his braces had surely gone into his tender lip. He probably had no idea that he'd cut himself, but when we kissed a second time he must have passed the teeniest, tiniest trace of blood to me, and now my throat was tightening and angry welts were rising on my skin.

I crumpled to the floor and tried to reach for my bag. Frenzied, Eli snagged my pack and opened it for me. I pawed around inside vainly before my vision blurred and went dark. I remember thinking that I must have only taken in a small amount of blood and that if Eli could get to my parents quickly, they could help me and everything would be fine this time. But I couldn't tell him. And I couldn't breathe. And everything was black and what I could hear sounded far away. Then suddenly, it didn't. I felt a cold pinch on my arm and I could inhale again. I opened my eyes and saw Eli, kneeling beside me, the cap of a syringe in his teeth, looking down in concentration at where he'd just injected me with medication. When he saw my eyes flutter open, an obvious sigh of relief escaped him.

"My hero," I croaked. "Lemme guess. You took a first-aid class for fun?"

"Boy Scout merit badge," he said. "Pretty sexy, right?" I smiled weakly at his joke. I didn't want to drift off. "I don't recognize this drug, though. What are you allergic to? Me?" I knew he was trying to make another joke, but the truth filled me with sadness. Basically, I *was* allergic to him. Because of how I now realized I felt, I was always going to want him to kiss me and he would always be helpless not to and there would always be the danger, however slight, of something like this happening again. And that would be just the beginning of our problems.

"It's complicated," I said, struggling to keep my eyes open and focused on him.

"How complicated could it be, Jane?" he asked, pushing my glasses back up my nose for me. "You could tell me anything. Anything. You know I would understand."

"Well," I sighed, "I hope you'll understand that I need you to go home now."

He frowned at me and shook his head. "Okay, that I don't understand. Why?" he asked.

"For starters, I'm going to crawl upstairs and pass out

for a while," I explained. "Then, when I wake up, I'm probably gonna have a hell of a case of diarrhea." Eli guffawed, thinking I was just trying to shock him. Boy, did I wish that were true.

"Can I help you up to your room?" he offered. I shook my head no, but I did allow him to assist me in getting on my feet. "Well, then I'll see you tomorrow, I guess."

I didn't want to lie to him, so I just said, "Thanks." I leaned back against the counter and clutched it with both hands to stay upright, as Eli picked up his skateboard. Part of me wanted him to leave as soon as possible, but another part of me wanted him to stay forever. I knew how dangerous wanting something to last forever could be. "But if you don't see me tomorrow, will you promise one thing?" I asked.

"Name it," he said.

"Don't go out with Astrid on Friday," I said, "or ever. She's not good. Not good enough for you."

Eli's face turned a deep shade of crimson and he rolled his eyes. "You dummy," he said. "I think I just said I'd go out with her to make you jealous. It was stupid. And mean. So, I guess I'm not good enough for me either."

"Well, then I guess you'll just have to stay home and not go out with yourself on Friday," I said, my balance wobbling as I tried to stay erect. "I'm sorry, I really have to lie down." Eli leaned in and kissed my forehead on what I could tell was probably a pulsating hive by the way he looked at it and cringed afterward. He went to the back door and let himself out, and even though I could barely stand, I hung on a little longer to watch him go.

# fifteen

**I pulled myself up the stairs on shaky legs, my backpack bumping as I dragged it behind me, and was surprised when I made it to the top.** While totally embarrassing, my allergic reaction wasn't as bad this time as I'd experienced in the past, maybe because of the mug of precious and rare blood I'd guzzled beforehand. I could already feel my skin starting to calm, thanks to Eli's quick thinking. He really was a good egg.

I wanted to go straight to my room and lie down, but when I reached my parents' door, I found myself knocking quietly and letting myself in. Ma was standing in the closet and my father was by the dresser. Their suitcases were open and half filled on top of the bed. I couldn't help noticing that between the pieces of luggage, there were also two foot-long pieces of lumber that had been sharpened into points. Had my parents always hidden stakes in their room in case a day like this ever came? My stomach lurched a bit. My mother turned to me with a stack of boxes in her hands. Boxes I'd seen her stash away on a high shelf just a few short months ago. "Sweetheart, you don't look so good," she said.

"I'm fine," I answered, though that was far, far, far from the truth. "Whatcha doin'?" Of course, I knew. I'd witnessed this scene so many times before, but never like this. Never with zero time to prepare.

My mother sighed sadly and put the boxes on the bed. "We're leaving. Much sooner than we'd hoped, but it can't be helped."

"We could stay and fight," I suggested. I couldn't believe I was saying it. The old me would never have dreamed of such a thing, but the new me wanted to put an end to the running, at least for now. I was ready to try something different.

"Jane," my mother replied, "we're just not that kind of people." Then she corrected herself. "We're not that kind of *vampire*. This isn't some novel or movie where the good vampires can beat the bad vampires if they're just willing to take a risk. Zach is in danger, and as his family, we have to protect him."

I swallowed, trying to force the sticky dryness down my throat. "How much time do we have left, then?" I asked.

"Your father's called in sick for his shift at the plant. If we work through the night, we could leave by morning. We'll take turns packing the car while someone watches your brother, so he's never alone. You can get some things together, but only what you absolutely need. Then you should get some rest. I'm sorry you won't have the chance to say goodbye to anyone, Jane." She touched my arm to comfort me and I let her.

"I don't want to say goodbye anyway," I said, looking deep into her eyes, then at my father, who'd continued folding his threadbare T-shirts in silence. For the first time since I'd come into the room, he met my eyes and I could tell that he felt ashamed. I hoped he could tell that I'd forgiven him. All it took was two minutes of believing that my baby brother might be lost forever for me to understand why he hadn't been able to face the possibility of watching me slip away. I went to him and put my face to his chest. He dropped the clothes in his hands, then hugged me so tightly, I thought my ancient bones would break. Finally, with some difficulty, I pushed myself away and took off my glasses to rub at my eyes, which felt like they were about to cry but had already run out of tears. I kissed my mother on her cool cheek and let myself out.

I stopped by my brother's room and he was hard at

work, mixing some formula and taking notes in a composition book. "Hey, kid," I said, "what's cookin'?"

"I just wanted to try something with the stuff I got today. I'm probably going to have to leave a lot of my materials behind," he said with a melancholy air. "Ma told me everything. I'm sorry. It's kinda my fault."

I punched him on the arm, but softly. "Don't you apologize or think for one second that any of this is your fault, okay?" I said. Then I brushed my hand through his crazy cowlick as he resumed stirring some bubbling liquid inside a beaker.

"Well, I want you to know that this is just a little setback," he told me, "and even though it's going to take a bit longer now, I'm still going to figure out a way for you to get better."

"Just be careful," I said.

"I know what I'm doing," he scoffed. I knew he believed I was telling him to be careful not to blow up his room, and I was, but I meant it in a more general sense too. I wanted him to stop worrying about me and take good care of himself. I looked down and caught myself wringing my hands as I struggled to hold my tongue. Add a robe, slippers, and a Volvo and I could have passed for a miniature version of Ma. Well, might as well just go with it. I bent and kissed his pale little nose, which caused him to rub at his face furiously with the back of his hand. I loved that little old kid.

I went to my room, turned on my heat lamps, and closed myself behind the thick curtains of my canopy bed. I could pack the minimal essentials later, but just then, I needed to lie down for a little while.

I tossed and turned for what felt like a few hours, drifting in and out of sleep that was filled with dreams that turned into nightmares. I didn't remember nearly dying of starvation and sickness, but if it was even slightly more unpleasant than how my night was proceeding, I was glad the memory was lost. Finally, I got up and clicked off the overhead lamps, allowing my eyes to adjust to the dark. The house felt still, but I was confident that one of my parents was watching over Zachary as the other tended to the errands that disappearing without a trace required.

I padded silently to my closet and opened it. I crammed two sweatshirts, two flannels, and two pairs of jeans into my backpack, along with a few pairs of socks and underwear from my drawer. I looked around to see if there was anything else I could or should take, but there was really nothing. I put on my sneakers and my glasses and sat down at my computer. I didn't bother checking my email or surfing the Web. I simply wiped my hard drive, then opened the word-processing program, and typed the following:

Dear Daddy and Ma,

When I learned earlier today that the
reason I am what I am is because you did
not want to let me go, I was more hurt and
angry than I have ever felt. Still, I'm not
proud of how I acted. I just wanted to let
you know that I'm not angry anymore,
because now I understand. I understand that
letting go of someone you love so much
probably feels worse than dying, or in our
case, worse than living forever. But I hope
that because you love me so much, you
might one day understand what I've decided
to do.

By the time you read this, I will be gone.
Not just gone away from here, but also gone
in the sense that I will no longer be the girl
you know. Not for long, anyway. I have a
once-in-a-long-long-lifetime opportunity to
change my fate and become a person again.
Ma, I know you said our life wasn't like a
novel or a movie where a good vampire
could win just by taking a risk, but I'm not
sure I completely agree with you. Winning is

a weird way to put it, anyway, especially
since I'll be losing a lot too, but I still think
it's a risk worth taking.

Please do not waste time looking for me.
This time it's my choice, and I've made up
my mind. I know that for Zach's sake you
cannot stay here, and I'm not certain when
or if I will see you again in my lifetime. But I
promise that I will never stop loving you or
looking for you for as long as I can, if you
promise never to forget me no matter how
much time passes.

Love, ~~Jane~~ Josephine

I left the document open on my desktop. Then I slowly
pulled the cord on my window's blackout shade, raising it
to reveal the dark sky beyond the glass. I undid the latch
at the top of the pane and slid the window open a foot or
so and threw my backpack to the ground, where it landed
with a soft plop on the grass. Carefully, I hoisted my legs
up and over the sill and slithered out feet-first, until my
sneakers were resting atop the portico covering our front
steps. I worried about making a noise that my parents, already on high alert, would come running in response to,

wielding flashlights and homemade stakes, but they didn't. I slid the window back down behind me, my transformation into a full-fledged sneak finally complete.

I worried that if someone was watching the house, they might have seen me slithering on my stomach down the porch roof, until my sneakers touched the damp mulch around our bushes. I wished there had been a way I could have locked the window behind me but reminded myself that even the evilest of vampires cannot turn into bats and fly. I was comforted by the notion that anyone trying to climb to that unlocked window would probably make a heck of a lot more noise going up than I had coming down.

I looked around and, seeing nothing out of the ordinary, picked up my backpack and started down my drive, moving quickly without looking back. The air was sufficiently cold that even my dry, chilly breath made faint clouds of condensation. I wrapped my arms around myself and trudged toward the train station. I wasn't planning to hop a freight anywhere. I was coming from the wrong side of the tracks, literally, and crossing the iron rails and wood ties was the fastest way to get to the side of town where oceanfront mansions loomed high on cliffs. I had taken my sweet time in giving Timothy an answer, and now I figured I'd better use a shortcut.

# sixteen

**I woke up just as I was about to fall off the edge of Timothy's king-size mattress.** It wasn't the first time in my life that I emerged from a foggy sleep needing a moment to remember exactly where I was, but it definitely was the first time I was waking up in a boy's bed. Or should I say a man's bed? Let's just say a guy's bed. However you put it, it was a huge step for me. I mean, true, the guy who owned the bed had slept downstairs somewhere in his huge mansion after bidding me sweet dreams, but did that make this occasion any less momentous? I didn't think so.

I opened the rich silk curtains surrounding me and hopped down from my nest, walking across the plush Oriental carpet in my bare feet to shut off Timothy's hot overhead lights. I thought about how he and I would experience many momentous things together after today. We'd experience all our momentous things together, I guessed, as I squinted at the fancy mahogany paneling that detailed the walls and made out the outline of the gigantic fireplace at the end of the room, big enough for me to stand up in. It was such an incredible house, unlike any I'd ever been inside. It was hard for me to believe that Timothy was willing to give it all up for me. Well, for us. I found my glasses on a dark wooden dresser and put them on while looking in a mirror, my face so plain, surrounded by an ornate gilt frame. I wondered if whatever place we'd live in together would be a millionth as beautiful as this house, or even my house. I wondered, when I was human again, how quickly my face would start to look older and if oranges and cinnamon cookies would smell delicious to me once more.

A soft knock at the door interrupted my thoughts. "Come in," I called.

Timothy entered, wearing driving loafers and khakis with a crisp shirt collar peeking out of the neck of his dark green wool knit pullover. He looked like a model from the catalogs I could never afford to order from. I suddenly became very self-conscious about my feet and whether or not they were weird-looking. I sat down in a damask slipper chair to unwad my wadded-up tube socks and put them on. I pulled my sneakers on without bothering to untie them.

"Did you rest well?" Timothy asked, bowing slightly toward me.

"Oh, I did," I said, "thank you. Thank you so much for letting me use your room and for . . . for . . . everything. Um, did you? Sleep well?"

"Yes, thank you," he replied. "I slept . . . oh, terribly, actually. I couldn't sleep at all. I was anxious for what today will bring. Excited. No need to hide it, right?"

I smiled. "Well, I wouldn't say I slept like a log either," I admitted. "But you know what they say, we can sleep when we're dead!" Oh, bravo, Jane. Excellent choice of words if you're trying to win a terrifying trophy at the Ominous Awards. I winced involuntarily at myself, but Timothy just chuckled dryly.

"Indeed we will," he said, "but that won't be for some time. Today, though, is a day that we'll remember for the rest of our lives, won't we?" With that, he held out his hand to me and led me from the room, like a gentleman who'd laid his jacket over a puddle for a lady. Very nice, but I had to put my other hand up to stifle some nervous laughter. I was really looking forward to the possibility of outgrowing this weird immature giggling thing I'd recently developed.

We spent the morning preparing for the arrival of Dr. Almos Erdos. Timothy explained that he'd sent the doctor a plane ticket to fly from Hungary to the United States and that if all had gone well, he should have touched down that morning. Dr. Erdos told Timothy he needed to rent a car at the airport because, while he was able to carry some of the ingredients for the compound cure he was hired to mix for us, he would have to pick up some supplies that he couldn't have brought aboard the plane without arousing suspicion. That made sense since, from what I understood, shampoo and toothpaste seemed to arouse suspicion at airports these days.

Once he was here and we'd said cheers, clinked glasses, and swigged this miracle elixir that would somehow reverse our undeadness, we were going to take his rental car back to the airport and choose a flight to hop on, while Dr. Almos Erdos stayed behind to receive the money from the new owner of Timothy's home, which would pay for the half of our treatment that hadn't already been covered by the cash deposit. Then we'd all live happily ever after. That was the plan.

As I helped Timothy put some clothes and personal items in matching leather bags, I couldn't help thinking of my family. I wondered how they'd reacted when they read my letter, and I tried to guess how far away they could be by now and in which direction they might have gone. I wished I had been able to give them some idea of where I was going, but if I'd given them even a shred of a clue, they would have delayed getting out of town and come looking for me, trying to stop me. I told myself over and over that I had done the right thing for all of us.

I noticed that Timothy didn't ask any questions about how I'd left things with my parents. Maybe he'd been alone for so long that he'd forgotten how much leaving someone you love hurts. Maybe he hadn't forgotten at all, and he didn't ask out of kindness for me. I didn't bring it up either, because I was sure that if I started telling the story, it wouldn't be long before I was spilling my guts about how my family were basically fugitives on the run from a psycho-killer vampire posing as a teacher at our school. I decided that, for now, I just had to have faith that they'd find a safe new place to start over. Just like I had to have faith that what Timothy and I were doing was going to work out for the best.

Once everything was done, Timothy and I sat in the front parlor at opposite ends of an old Chippendale sofa, watching the mantel clock tick forward into the gray afternoon. I caught Timothy looking at me once, but when he noticed that I noticed, he looked away nervously. My guts twisted, as I hoped with all my heart that my normally cool companion was not already second-guessing his decision to join humanity with me. I was mentally trying to will him to speak at that minute or forever hold his peace when the clock struck two, and a split second later, the doorbell chimed. Timothy looked at me and held out his hand, maybe just a little less gracefully than he had that morning, and together we went to the large oak door. Timothy unlocked the deadbolt, turned the knob, and opened the door, and in walked a man so tall, ample, pink, and smiling that I could not help smiling myself.

"Hello! You must be Timosee," he laughed with his thick accent, pumping Timothy's arm up and down with his own substantial hand in an enthusiastic shake. "And you," he said, turning to me and spreading his great arms wide for a hug, "you must be Chane." As he squeezed me to his expansive chest, I turned my head and widened my eyes at Timothy, whose own eyes were dancing with repressed laughter. "It is wery nice to finally meet bose of you."

"It's very nice to meet you as well, Dr. Erdos," said Timothy as he hefted the man's trunk from outside the door. "Where can I put this for you?"

"Ah, I sink ze kitchen vould be best," he said. "Und, please, ve are frents. Call me Almos." Timothy nodded respectfully, then hoisted the case onto his shoulder and led the way to the back of the house.

The kitchen, like the rest of the house, was magnificent, with more ovens, sinks, and racks of shiny copper pots than I think even the most ambitious home cook could realistically make use of. Which was kind of sad, considering that not so much as a Hot Pocket had probably been prepared there in at least a few years. Timothy set the trunk down on the marble surface of the center island and said, "I'm afraid I didn't think to shop for any refreshments to offer you. There might be some tea somewhere. . . ."

Dr. Erdos dismissed him with a raised hand. "Hup, please. You mustn't vorry about me. I am here for ze two of you." He beamed, turning to me. "And vhen ve are done, perhaps ve can share some tea togezzer! Does zat sound nice?" I smiled as he patted his substantial belly and exclaimed, "Or maybe ve get a burger, hmm? Ve'll see." He snapped open the brass latches on his case and opened it to reveal a portable laboratory, which he began carefully unpacking and meticulously assembling on the counter before him. "Shall ve begin?"

Timothy and I nodded gravely. Dr. Erdos started fiddling with a few pieces of apparatus for a minute before slapping himself on the forehead and turning to Timothy. "Actually," he said sheepishly, "before ve begin, vould you mind making ze partial payment . . . as ve discussed?" I could tell he felt awkward, bringing up such matters, but business was business.

"Of course," Timothy said earnestly. He excused

himself, then returned quickly with a bundle wrapped in brown paper and tied with twine. "I could open it and count it if you'd like."

Dr. Erdos waved his hands frantically. "No, no," he proclaimed, "I trust. I trust." Slipping the package into his briefcase, he resumed his work.

Timothy and I watched as the doctor carefully weighed and measured, mixed and boiled the precious and scarce elements of his revolutionary formula. I couldn't help thinking how much Zachary would have gotten a kick out of seeing this big, nutty guy humming and dancing as he worked, like a chef composing his signature soup. He sang softly to himself, "La da da da dee, and ve are almost zere." Then he paused midstir and said to me, "Ach, Chane, I nearly forgot. Timosee informs me zat you are a unique wampire. Is true you are allergic to blood?"

I nodded reluctantly. "I'm blood-intolerant."

"Zo, if you feed on ze blood vhat happens to you?" he asked.

"Um, if I accidentally ingest any blood, other than this rare type called Bombay, which is really difficult to get, as well as incredibly expensive, I have a severe reaction. Throat closes, skin bubbles up . . . Uh, there's some . . . intestinal distress." I didn't dare look at Timothy, but Dr. Erdos's expression was pained enough. Suddenly, a terrible thought occurred to me. "Why? Does that mean that this won't work on me?" Dr. Erdos drew in a big breath and paused for an excruciating moment before answering.

"No. It vill vork. It vill vork. But," he said, "do you have any medications zat you take vhen you have zis reaction?"

"Yes," I said, "I always carry it with me. I left my bag upstairs, but I have some in there."

"Okay." He grinned warmly. "Might be good idea if you have medicine wiz you, on infinitesimal chance zat somesing goes little bit wrong, no?"

I tried not to look alarmed as I backed out of the kitchen to run upstairs and get my backpack. A few minutes later I was back with my bag as Dr. Erdos swirled a smoking purple liquid in a flask, then poured it into two separate test tubes in equal amounts. He turned to Timothy and me, saying, "Vhen zees babies turn clear in few minutes, ve vill be ready to rock und roll!" He clapped his hands together excitedly as the three of us kept our eyes trained on the tubes.

*Bee-boop. Bee-boop.* A noise that I assumed came from some timer or electronic meter in the doctor's kit went off. Timothy tapped my shoulder, saying, "Jane, I think your bag's ringing." I listened again and opened my front pouch where my cell phone sat, with a flashing messages icon. No wonder I hadn't recognized the alert. I don't think anyone had ever left me a message since I'd first gotten the phone a few months ago. I was mad at myself for even having the phone with me now. I'd intended to leave it behind in my room so that I wouldn't be tempted to try to contact my family if I had second thoughts, but obviously it had slipped my mind. It seemed like my family had been trying frantically to contact me all day too. Out of thirty-two missed calls, thirty-one were from my home number. The thirty-second number was one I didn't recognize immediately. I thought it was probably my parents again, hopefully calling from somewhere on the road, and I considered just erasing it, but then something, perhaps my vampire instincts kicking in one last time, told me to listen to it. I pressed the button and held the phone up to my ear. I recognized the voice instantly.

"Hey, Lame," Astrid jibed. "I found something that belongs to you, but if you don't want it, I know someone who's dying to have it." Then there was some background noise and her now-muffled voice said, "Tell her."

I moaned. Timothy and Dr. Erdos looked at me with worry. I covered my mouth to stifle a desperate whimper as I heard my brother's voice, small and afraid.

"Jane, when Dad and Ma told me you weren't coming with us, I snuck away to try to find you. I thought you went to school to see Eli. I just wanted to say goodbye,

Jane. I'm sorry if I messed everything up—" The muffled sounds returned, and then Astrid was back on the line.

"I know you're with Timothy and I know what you're doing," she hissed. "If the two of you don't show up at the school, I'm going to deliver you-know-what to you-know-who for you-don't-even-want-to-*know*-what. You've got till four o'clock. And you both better still be vampires when you get here." The message ended. I tried to hang up, but the phone fell from my numb fingers.

"We have to go," I said to Timothy.

"What? Where?" Timothy asked, confused.

"Astrid knows everything. She has my brother and he's in danger," I wailed. "I would go by myself, but she's demanding that both of us meet her at school before we take the cure. She said to be there by four o'clock or . . ." I couldn't go on. Timothy turned to Dr. Erdos.

"Doctor," he said, his voice thick with reluctance, "will you wait here for us until we get back?"

The doctor ran his hands through his disheveled mop of curly hair and shook his head, gesturing to the two test tubes, the contents of which were now nearly clear. "I am afraid," he explained, "zat if you do not take ze cure within ze hour, it loses its . . . efficacy. It becomes . . ." He struggled to come up with the most scientifically accurate word. "It becomes junk!"

Timothy looked from the doctor to me. I could tell he was loathe to run out of his house to help me save a little vampire kid he'd never even met while our window of opportunity quickly shrunk, but I was ready to pick him up and throw him over my shoulder if I had to. "I'm sorry," I said. "But we have to go save my brother first. If you care about me at all, you will come now!" I grabbed my bag and started for the door, then turned back to see Timothy, still standing where he'd been, dumbfounded. I shouted, "Timothy, please! If we don't both show up, Astrid is going to do something really bad to Zachary."

Timothy opened his mouth to speak to the doctor, possibly to ask him to talk some sense into me, but Almos Erdos, obviously sympathetic to my intense state of distress, spoke first.

"Go," he boomed, sweeping his shovel-size hand toward the door. "Go, go! I come wiz you." He scanned his work area, then grabbed two black rubber stoppers that he shoved into the tops of the glass test tubes, which he carefully transferred to the inner pocket of his sport coat. He glanced at the big octagonal face of his digital watch and announced, "Ve have ezzactly fifty-sewen minutes."

# seventeen

**I flew through the front doors of Port Lincoln High without looking back to see if Timothy and Dr. Erdos were keeping up.** The slap of my sneakers echoed off the walls in the dim and deserted entrance hall. I charged up the stairs two at a time, never letting up despite the burning in my atrophied legs. When I got to the doorway of Ms. Smithburg's class, I saw Astrid's long, shimmering waves but could not see my brother. As soon as I threw open the door, Astrid jerked around to face me, and there was Zach, his neck squeezed under her arm with his own scrawny wrists bound behind his back. "Jane," he rasped, "I'm sorry. I'm sorry."

A moment later, Timothy pelted into the room with Dr. Erdos right behind, gulping and gasping and clutching his weathered briefcase with one hand and his chest with the other. I remembered what it felt like to have a pounding heart and was glad for once that mine could not.

Astrid's perfectly glossed lips broke open into a vulgar grin that revealed her perfectly glistening white fangs. "Jane," she exclaimed in faux surprise, "you came! And you brought friends! How sweet."

"Astrid," I commanded, "let him go." She tightened her hold on Zach's throat, causing him to make a strangled gagging noise. I looked to Timothy and Dr. Erdos. Astrid was certainly a more powerful vampire than I, but between the three of us, surely we could take her. Or could we? Perhaps Timothy and I put together were no match for Astrid, and Dr. Erdos was just a person. There was even a risk that he would be bitten, and that his incredible formula for curing vampirism could die with him. Still, I thought we should go for it and I tried to convey my idea to Almos and Timothy with my eyes, but it was Astrid who could read me. She scanned the desks around her and snatched up a sharpened pencil, aiming the point directly at my brother's heart. Funny, it had never occurred to me that I should be afraid of pencils, but now that I thought about it, they were nothing more than little wooden stakes you could write with. I dropped the idea of overpowering her.

"What do you want?" I asked.

"I just want what you want, Jane," she replied, trying to sound innocent. "It didn't take a genius to figure out what you and Timothy were up to." Well, that was obvious now.

"And when I put two and two together and realized today was the big day, I said to myself, 'Ya know what? I'll have what she's having!'" She tilted her head to me, awaiting my response, but it was Timothy who spoke up.

"Astrid," he said, gently, "I know I've hurt you, and I can see that you're upset. Why don't you let Jane's brother go, and you and I can discuss it." He reached his hand toward her, nervously, but still much like a prince offering to dance with a lady. Astrid scoffed. It was not attractive.

"Shut up, Timothy," she sneered. "And stop flattering yourself. I'm not doing this because I looooove you," she said, glowering. "I'm doing this because I hate Jane. Little Miss Perfect Vampire with the loving family and the great grades plus an undead *and* a real live boy falling all over themselves to be with her. She simply can't tolerate drinking one drop of blood and she has a fake eating disorder! Poor baby." It was no surprise that Astrid hated me, but when I heard the reasons why, it actually sounded like she was kind of jealous. Of me! I would have liked to enjoy that feeling for a second, but Astrid's testy tirade wasn't over just yet.

"Everybody else might be buying your bull, Jones, but not me. I was in the middle of trying to come up with a brilliant plan to wreck *your* brilliant plan, when your dumb little brother fell right into my lap. What's his name? Zach?

Well, I like to call him Chip, because he's my little bargaining chip." Astrid gave Zach's neck another squeeze for effect, then laughed as Dr. Erdos raised his eyebrows at Timothy. I tried to think of what I should do, inching backward toward the teacher's anteroom office, wondering if there was something, anything in there that I could use.

Astrid continued her assault, saying, "Honestly, Tim, I don't give a shit what happens to you. I just want the cure and you're gonna give it to me or I'm gonna give Jane's brother to someone who's going to do very bad things to him." I froze as everyone's eyes turned to me to see how I would respond. I tried to sound tough.

"Astrid," I said, "I didn't know it was possible for someone to be a vampire and a witch. But that's what you are. A witch. *But with a* B." I wasn't sure, but despite his terrible position, I thought I saw Zach actually roll his eyes at that one. Astrid didn't seem as rattled as I'd hoped either, but before she could reply, a loud bang startled us all as the door behind me burst open. I never had a chance to turn and see who it was, but from the hands that had suddenly wrapped around my throat, I got a pretty good idea. Then I heard her voice and I knew for sure.

"Welcome to my class, everyone," said Ms. Smithburg. Ruth Pike. Besides the choking, I felt a cold jabbing a few inches below my jaw. I strained my eyes to see the source, and once they focused, I could see that my American history teacher was holding a syringe filled with red fluid. Blood. Probably not the rare Bombay blood that I drank in small amounts to survive either. I was guessing it was just the regular kind of blood that I was allergic to. Even if I had thought to bring in the bag with my medicine in it, which was still sitting on the backseat of Dr. Erdos's rental car, the amount of blood aimed at my jugular looked sufficient to render me incapacitated in a pretty bad way. Probably worse off than old Turner Pike.

So, this was great. Out of six people in a room, the two of us who were Joneses were both in headlocks with deadly implements aimed at us. It was something of a standoff. Astrid looked like she was about to have a temper tantrum.

"What are you doing here?" she shrieked at Ms. Smithburg. "I told you I would take care of it!"

"I know you did," Ms. Smithburg replied, "but I have trust issues. Forgive me, dear. I'll take young Mr. Jones off your hands now." But Astrid didn't budge. Now the allies looked like enemies too.

"You were right not to trust her," I croaked. "She was never going to give him to you." Timothy and Dr. Erdos looked at me, wild-eyed. At some point, both of them had put their hands up like this was a bank robbery. It wasn't exactly confidence-inspiring.

"Lame's right," Astrid hissed. "I know I told you that I would help you get the kid, because I wanted to stick it to his dear, dear sister. But then I thought, *What's in it for me?* I don't even take American history, so it's not like you can even give me an A for my trouble. Even if you could, it's not like I care about my grades, right? Then, when I figured out that Jane and Timothy were cashing in his fortune to pay for this doctor's cure for vampirism, I decided I wanted that and the brat was the perfect way to get it."

I couldn't see Ms. Smithburg's face, but I could feel her rapid exhalation on the top of my head as she said, "A cure? For vampirism? That cannot be."

Dr. Erdos spoke for the first time since he'd entered the room. "No, it is true. I have been vorking many years and my treatment is effectiff." I'd have preferred it if he'd saved the sales pitch for another time, but I guess I couldn't blame him for being psyched about his discovery. He continued, "Is prohibitively expensive for many of your kind, but Timosee"—he nodded to Timothy—"was able to come up with ze necessary funds for two doses, for him und young Chane." Then, ever so slightly, it felt like Ms. Smithburg loosened her grip around my neck.

"But Jane is sick with a rare condition. Did she tell you

that?" Ms. Smithburg asked Dr. Erdos. For a second, I thought the woman who was threatening to end me had a change of heart and was now trying to protect me. Only for a second, though. Until Dr. Erdos nodded and replied.

"Ze treatment offers complete rewersal of the wampirism," he explained. "It restores the subject to the same degree of health zey enchoyed as human." I knew word of mouth was the best advertising, but I really started to wish that Dr. Almos Erdos would shut his big one. He smiled patronizingly at Ms. Smithburg and she slackened her grip even further. Then she remembered herself and clamped down on my neck tighter than ever.

"Then give it to me," she said, "and I'll let *young Jane* go." Timothy looked at me, but I had nothing for him. This was a lose-lose situation. Actually, it might have been a lose-lose-lose situation, if that was possible. Timothy's shoulders sagged and he gestured in resignation to Ms. Smithburg.

"Give it to her," Timothy said to Dr. Erdos, who reacted with a look of utter shock. "Do it!" As Dr. Erdos carefully withdrew the two glass vials from the safety of his jacket's inner pocket, Astrid's face crumpled into a mask of bitter hatred.

"What?" Astrid wailed. "You have got to be effing kidding me!" I swiveled my head to see my baby brother, still completely at Astrid's mercy, and she frankly didn't look all that merciful right now. I mouthed a silent prayer that an opportunity to rescue Zach would present itself, and fast.

As Dr. Erdos proffered the test tubes to my captor, she flung the syringe of blood to the floor and released me with a violent shove. I fell in a heap at Timothy's feet, fighting to catch my breath. We all watched in awe as Ms. Smithburg held the two glass tubes in either hand. She used her fangs to uncork one and drank the entire contents in one greedy gulp. I glanced briefly around the room and couldn't help noticing that even though things had gone horribly wrong for us, Dr. Erdos looked weirdly thrilled. His eyes were wide and he beamed as he clapped his beefy hands together in anticipation. Then the sound of breaking glass recaptured my attention as Ms. Smithburg tossed the empty vessel on the floor, where it burst into tiny glittering splinters of glass. She wiped at her mouth with the back of her hand and gave a throaty, evil chuckle.

"I hate to drink and run," Ms. Smithburg said, "but if you'll excuse me, I'll be bringing this home to my husband." She held the second tube aloft and the late-afternoon sun shone through the clear solution inside.

"Oh, no," Dr. Erdos said, cutting short Ms. Smithburg's moment of triumph. All of our eyes turned to him. "I'm afraid zere isn't time for you to go anyvhere. Unless you can get to him wizin—" The doctor checked his watch. "Wizin eight minutes? Othervise, it vill no longer be effectiff." For a second I stared at her, wondering how she would react. I knew that she knew there was no way she could make it to Fairhaven within eight minutes. Then I remembered to give Dr. Erdos a super-dirty look for not just letting her go. He shrugged at me as if to say, *Sorry, Chane. I'm un blabbermouse.* I shook my head in disbelief.

"Tough luck, Teach." Astrid's mood had vastly improved in the last few seconds, because she'd seen her opportunity. "Interested in making a trade?"

"No!" I shouted, but it was futile. I watched in horror as Astrid lowered the pencil from where she'd been poking Zach in his ribs and handed him over to Ms. Smithburg in exchange for the remaining vial of Dr. Erdos's cure. Ms. Smithburg held my brother in front of her tightly, as if he was shielding her from imminent danger. Astrid pulled the rubber stopper out of the vial and held it up.

"I'd like to propose a toast," Astrid brayed. "To Timothy and Jane and the good doctor who made this all possible. I think what I'm going to do is drink this, right? Then, I'm going to take off for Hollywood and become a famous actress. Then, after six or seven years, when I'm in my prime, I'm going to go vampire again. Ha-ha! I'm going revamp! Then, I'll be eternally beloved *and* hot. . . ."

For someone who only had a few minutes to play with, Astrid sure was taking her ridiculous time before drinking the damn thing. Obviously, she was ramping up the drama. I hated to admit it, but she probably *would* make a great actress. I tore my attention away from Astrid's spontaneous monologue to check on my poor little brother. Intent on coming up with a last-ditch plan to get him away from Ms. Smithburg, it took me a moment to realize what I was seeing. And what I was seeing was something incredible.

The arm that Ms. Smithburg had wound around Zachary's throat was no longer alabaster and smooth. It was dark. Black, in fact. And was that faint smoke rising from the surface of her skin? I blinked my eyes to make sure I wasn't hallucinating, but it was true. As everyone was watching Astrid ham it up, I was watching a horrific color creep up Ms. Smithburg's arm, while the ends of her fingers took on the look of a burnt log in a fireplace, right before the embers collapse into ash.

"So, bottoms up!" Astrid concluded, and made a big show of raising the test tube higher, then bringing it to her lips. Impulsively, I sprang up and slapped the vial out of Astrid's hand, spilling its entire contents as it crashed to the floor. Astrid roared and lunged at me, but I dodged her blow.

"Zachary!" I yelled. "Run!" For a brief moment, my brother looked at me, confused; then he put his head down and threw his weight against Ms. Smithburg's cruel embrace. A cracking noise rang out and we all stood in stunned awe as her blackened arms snapped off like brittle branches and clattered to the floor, then crumbled. Astrid forgot all about trying to murder me as Ms. Smithburg's body, inch by inch, rapidly became petrified, then desiccated. The affliction traveled up her neck and she was able to see with her own still-working eyes as the lower part of her face became coal-like, then broke away. When the transformation was complete, Ms. Smithburg's figure stood there for a moment, resembling a wooden mannequin or totem that had been burned; then she fell into a mound of dust.

Astrid looked from the pile to me to Timothy and back to the pile, breathing through her mouth without speaking. I'm sure she was just trying to think of the nicest possible way to say, "Thanks for saving my miserable life, Jane. You really shouldn't have."

I hugged Zach to my chest with one arm, and reached my other arm out to take Timothy's hand and squeeze it. It was impossible to look away from the heap of cinders that was once Ms. Smithburg. We stared in disbelief, when suddenly, the top layer of my powdered history teacher began to swirl and dance as if it were still somehow alive. But it was only being blown by a breeze from an open window. A window that Dr. Almos Erdos had opened sometime during the chaos. A window that Dr. Almos Erdos had used to escape.

# eighteen

**Timothy and I ran to the open window** in what was the former Ms. Smithburg's former classroom just in time to see the nondescript rental car that had driven us to the school scream out of the parking lot with Almos Erdos (probably not his real name) at the wheel.

I barely had the courage to look Timothy in the eye. If it weren't for me showing him that ridiculous Internet article in the first place, we never would have gotten mixed up with a phony doctor who claimed to have discovered the cure for vampirism, when what he'd actually invented was "liquid stake." When I put two and two together, based on his delight at Ms. Smithburg's ingestion of his potion and his quick escape once it had vaporized her, it was now obvious to me that he was a freelance vampire hunter who was out to find a couple of bloodsucking suckers and kill them, while making a quick bundle of cash to boot.

On the other hand, if it weren't for that article and a big

chunk of Timothy's fortune, my family would be fleeing for Zach's life now. My emotions were mixed, but my guilt was full strength.

"I'm so sorry," I whispered hoarsely, staring at the empty lot below. Timothy put his hand under my chin and raised my face. He grabbed the sides of my head and leaned in, pressing his full frigid lips to my forehead. The wave of energy that passed from him to me was complex, and I could pick out notes of sorrow and disappointment and maybe even a bit of relief. We gazed at each other, ignoring Astrid's haughty and snotty muttering across the room.

"I'm going to follow him, Jane," Timothy said, "so he doesn't try to do this to anyone else. I don't know when I'll be back, but I hope you'll be here." I nodded and watched as he slid out the window and scrabbled down the fire escape in pursuit of the Hungarian murderer and swindler. Then he was gone.

I turned away from the window, and my little brother, Zach, gave one of those half smiles that isn't really happy at all but is used to convey pity. I was feeling slightly pitiful, so I was more than grateful to accept. Astrid, on the other hand, wasn't feeling quite so generous.

"FYI, you still make me sick," Astrid informed me. "And all of this doesn't mean we're friends, got it?"

I got it loud and clear. I'd saved her life, but she would

continue to make mine as miserable as she could. I didn't even bother saying a word to her as she left the room, though perhaps with a bit less swagger than she once had. Perhaps.

I knelt behind Zach and worked on freeing his hands, which were bound behind his back with strong athletic tape. Once he was loose, I stood up and rubbed his wrists, then hugged him, then leaned back to look at his cute little face, then hugged him again. It was when we were hugging for the second time that we heard the unmistakable *squeak, squeak, squeak* of sneakers running down the hallway and past our door. A second later, the squeaking stopped, then reversed back toward us just as quickly, until the footwear in question was planted in the doorway, and standing there inside it was Eli Matthews. He let out a small whoop of relief.

"Eli, what are you doing here?" I asked, shocked to see him. He held up a freckled finger to ask for my patience while he gulped at the air. Then, slightly winded, he began.

"After . . . after what happened yesterday (pant, pant) in your kitchen, and when . . . and when you didn't make it to school today, I was (deep breath) I was worried," he said, gradually regaining his composure. "So, I swung by your house . . . after school. And your parents . . . your parents were freaking out . . . because they said you and

Zach were both missing." He put a hand up to his chest, as if he could slow his rapidly beating heart by stroking it like a cat. "So, I offered to help them look for you."

"My parents are out looking for us?" I asked, my voice cracking with emotion I hadn't expected to feel.

"They're downstairs," Eli said, "in the car." I put my hands gently on my brother's shoulders and steered him toward the door.

"Go get in the car with Dad and Ma and tell them we're okay," I instructed. "Try to explain everything that happened. I've got some things to take care of, but I'll be home as soon as I can." Zach looked at me like he was afraid to let me out of his sight, but I was firm. "Go now. I will see you later."

"Jane, I—" Zach paused and tilted his head awkwardly like he sometimes did when he was trying to think of how to put something.

"You love me?" I said. "You better."

Zach bobbled and wobbled like ten-year-old kids do, and I gave him a silent wave to let him know I was serious about him getting out of there. He put his head down and dashed out of the room, leaving me alone with Eli. I got a wastebasket from the front of the room and started picking up shards of glass and tossing them in, careful to avoid any blood or drops of Dr. Erdos's potion, just in case.

"So," Eli said after a moment, "is the paper I wrote so bad that you thought you'd better do some after-school suck-up cleaning for extra credit?" He looked around at the bits of test tube and syringe, and the heap of soot that he had no idea was the remnants of our American history teacher, and shook his head. "What the h-e-double-hockey-sticks even happened in here?"

"It's a long story," I said, "and the paper you wrote was really good. It doesn't have anything to do with all this." Then I thought about it and corrected myself. "Well, it kind of has something to do with it, but not like . . . It's— it's insanely complicated." I frowned at him, but only because I wished I could have given him a better answer.

I crouched down and started scooping ashes into the garbage with my bare hands. Eli went to Ms. Smithburg's coat closet at the front of the room and retrieved a dustpan and brush. I shivered as I caught a glimpse of her long, elegant coat still hanging inside the door, then looked down at my dusty hands and shivered again. I rubbed them on my jeans and watched as Eli began methodically and efficiently sweeping up the rest.

"You know," he said, "you can tell me anything. You can. You can trust me, Jane."

Trusting someone wasn't something I'd tried to do much in the past, and even though my most recent experiment with trust had been a big fat failure, I couldn't help wondering if I could trust this boy. Was he ready to hear the secrets that I had? Was I ready to tell him? Was he the kind of guy who would be cool with learning that he just helped me clean up the remains of my enemy, the vampire teacher? Would he be down with helping me sneak into a church, liberate an old priest from the bonds of her psychic trance, and then bury the sick undead body of her groom where nobody would ever find him? If my blood-intolerance was ever cured, would he still be willing to kiss me, if he knew that I probably had at least ten years on his great-grandmother? It was kind of a lot to ask of someone. Eli eyed me hopefully, waiting for me to speak.

"Thanks," I answered. I was afraid that if I said anything more, everything would come tumbling out before I had a chance to stop it. Then Eli reminded me of one of the best things about him: when you didn't feel like talking, he talked enough for both of you.

"Okay," he said, "so, I told Astrid that I can't go out with her tomorrow. She seemed mad, but not just mad at me. It was more like she was mad at everything. She's kind of a monster. Anyway, now that I'm free tomorrow, I was wondering if you wanted to do something—as friends, no pressure—we could go to a movie or, if you're not feeling confident about our project, we could work on that. . . ."

"I wouldn't worry about the project," I said.

"Really?" He sounded kind of flattered. "You think I nailed it?"

"Something like that," I said.

"So, a movie then?" he resuggested.

"I don't know," I replied. "Do you like Jimmy Stewart?"

"Are you kidding?" he said. "Jimmy Stewart is my boy! I have *The Philadelphia Story* on DVD. Have you seen it?" Eli trailed off into a long explanation of why James Maitland Stewart was—in his humble opinion—the finest American actor in history.

So I wasn't a human girl again like I thought I was going to be, but who could predict the future? I sure couldn't. Maybe I needed to just try to relax and enjoy what I had right now. Because for the first time in a long time, I felt like I had some choices I could make in my life and I was ready to make one.

I decided that when I got home and logged on to my computer, I would find Eli Matthews's friend request and just accept it.

# ACKNOWLEDGMENTS

I owe about a million thank-yous to about a million people who helped me become the author of my first real-live novel. There's Arjun Basu, who said he liked my idea, and Alan Katz, who is *the* person to talk to when you have an idea, because he is *the* most fantastic idea guy.

I want to thank Josh and Tracey Adams of Adams Literary for believing I could write a book and for helping *me* believe I could write a book, and my editor, Shana Corey, at Random House for her imagination and for all her excellent, expert advice and care. I could not have asked for kinder, smarter, more thoughtful people to guide me on my way.

I owe thanks to many, many friends, but especially Dave Holmes and Lisa Jane Persky, who both knew what I was up to, and checked in on me regularly to make sure

I was keeping it up. Thanks to Paul F. Tompkins and Nelson Walters for making me laugh my head off all the time and for being what I will always consider "my team." I could go on forever thanking pals who inspire and encourage me every day, but I'm afraid I'd run out of room! So for now I'll just say thanks to all of my friends, both in real life and not-exactly-real life, for being your irreplaceable selves.

A special thank-you goes to my high school English teacher, Ms. Melanie Gallo. I hope that everyone is lucky enough to have a teacher at least once in their life who will lend them a book to read from her own private collection, not for an assignment, but just because she thought they would love it.

There are a few people whom I could never thank enough, but I will try. Karen and Roger Debenham, thank you for being the greatest in-laws in recorded history. Thank you to my mom, Donna St. Onge, for always telling me I should write a book and for being proud of me when I did. To Matt, Eli, and Lincoln, I thank you for being a family more patient, generous, funny, and wise than I ever could have dreamed of having. You are the best eggs in the basket.